The Queen of All Magick

Elizabeth

By

Kathi S. Barton

World Castle Publishing, LLC

WCP

World Castle Publishing, LLC
Pensacola, Florida

ISBN: 9781629890760
First Edition World Castle Publishing, LLC, March 28, 2014
http://www.worldcastlepublishing.com

Cover: Karen Fuller
Editor: Eric Johnston

CHAPTER 1

Duncan held the wet cloth over the wound and felt his heart race. He'd done it again, failed in his duties as a babysitter. He was terrified beyond anything he'd ever done before. Even wrecking the nice, new car last month, which had not been his fault, had not frightened him as much as this.

"I shall have the doctor look at it as soon as the sun sets more. He will need to take you to the clinic, I have no doubt. You should know that I am so very sorry, Master Mathew. I should have watched you more closely."

"Mr. Duncan, I keep telling you I just need a bandage. I swear, nobody's gonna care that I scraped my knee. Look at this." He pulled up his shirt and showed him the wide gash along his torso. "Mom said it was amazing."

Duncan grabbed the chair behind him, forgetting to be nervous about the blood on the washcloth for several seconds. He looked at the wound and tried to understand how Master Mathew was not in surgery right now. Duncan felt the master touch his mind.

"You all right there, Duncan? I can feel your fear. Is watching little Mathew for a few hours becoming too much for you?" Duncan bristled, and the master laughed. *"Shall we come there and rescue you?"*

"You most certainly will not. I have things under control. Master Mathew has torn his knee open again and I'm aiding him now." He felt laughter again. *"He will require someone to have a look at his chest as well. It seems that Miss Lizzy has left him to get all sorts of wounds under her care. There is a wound on his chest that looks as if he has been playing with your swords again. And I did not allow it despite you saying he would be fine. He is not fine."*

"The small scrape on his chest? I saw that. Lizzy said he got it trying to save a kitten. Damn near got himself stuck too, but the little cat is fine. You should see the little feline. Fell for me on sight." Duncan thought there were few females, no matter what the species, that would not like the master.

"Be that as it may, my lord, but he is injured again. I have tried to reason with him, but he says that a bandage will fix it properly. I've a call to Sir Thomas when he wakes for the evening. I was thinking to take the young master to the human hospital, but he said he'd have a bloody cow if I did. I do wonder where he gets such comments." Duncan watched as Mathew turned on the tap in the sink, wet a paper towel, and pressed it against his knee. When he was satisfied with the wound, he jumped down off the counter and ran toward the door, which had Duncan thinking the boy needed to wear padding around his body to keep him safe. He ran out to do who knew what to get him injured again.

"Duncan, you've become an old woman. And we both know that he mimics every word his grandmother says to him. I've tried my best to tell him it's wrong, but you know how things go." Duncan started to argue that he was the one the child was mimicking but was cut off. *"You'll have to learn to relax or when the other two children come, you'll be a mess. Just take a deep breath and tell Mathew to go out and play. He'll be fine."*

Other children. He'd forgotten about them. Miss Lizzy and Master Logan had been saying that the children of the home were coming soon and they were preparing for them. That was why he had Master Mathew today, so that they might have the home prepared in time.

"How will she manage with all of them bent on getting injured daily?" Duncan thought about blocking his lordship but didn't. He was having entirely too much fun at his expense, and Duncan was not happy with it. When the room tightened, he thought for sure that he was coming to investigate the wound, but it was Lady Elizabeth, the queen's mother.

"You needed me?" He'd forgotten that he'd summoned her when Mathew had entered the house for lunch sporting the large patch of blood in his torn jeans. "Duncan, what have you done here? Are you planning to perform surgery?"

He started to gather the large first-aid kit he'd purchased several days ago. The advertisement had said it was equipped with everything needed to take care of a family of five. Duncan now despaired of it caring for one small human boy. Sitting down, Duncan looked at her ladyship.

"I do believe that I am a failure as a sitter, my lady. Every time young Master Mathew comes here I feel as if it will be the last." Lady Elizabeth sat down across from him, and a glass of his favorite sherry was in front of him. "Thank you. I should not partake when he is on the premises, but I feel as if I've been run through the dryer."

"Ringer. And I know what you mean. It's hard to see to children now days." She reached for her own glass and drank it down, much to his amazement. "I've needed this for days. I just never…have I ever told you how I was made? Or by whom?"

"No, my lady, you have not. I have heard that someone, a very powerful being created you, but nothing more. He did a wonderful job of it if you were to ask me." She nodded, but Duncan knew she was distracted. "My lady, is there anything I may do for you?"

"I don't want to miss you all, and I will. Especially you, my dear friend." Duncan sat there speechless for a long time as she simply looked out the window over the kitchen. He knew that she had come back some time ago, just when Lady Sara had come to his lordship. But he had thought her to be happy. And she seemed to enjoy the new grandchildren that the queen and king now had. All seven of them.

"I'm sorry, Duncan, you must think I'm an old fuddy." He had no idea what that was but doubted very much that it described her. When the door to the kitchen opened and Mathew came tumbling in, Duncan stood up to see what harm had befallen him again. But the little boy launched himself at his grandmother and held her tightly. Duncan smiled at the two of them.

"I've not seen you in a while, Grams. Whatcha been up to?" Mathew sat down in the chair across from them both as he continued. "I came in for something to eat and here you are. This is the best kind of lunch date."

The little boy was a charmer. If Duncan didn't know better, he'd swear he was related to his lordship by blood and not by marriage. Mathew belonged to Master Logan and Miss Lizzy was his stepmother, but you'd never know by the way they got along. Duncan got up to make him some lunch as the two of them talked. When his lordship spoke again, Duncan wasn't really surprised.

"Tell the scamp that I'm on my way up now. He's been bugging me for a chance to see the new books I got for us."

Duncan turned to tell the young master that when his lordship continued. *"Do you think his mother would mind overly much if I took him with me today? I have that meeting that I must attend. His father will be there."*

"I do not believe she thinks young Mathew is a good influence on you. She seems to think that the two of you get into more mischief than when apart. Miss Lizzy has said to me that you are being bamboozled, and quite well too." Duncan laughed when his lordship sputtered. Again he had no idea what that word meant; but he was happy to see that it rendered his master speechless. When the master came through the door a few minutes later, Duncan could see that the man was as in love with the young man as he was his own mate. And that was never a bad thing.

"I've a meeting today with your dad. He is going to show me where we can build the new fire department. Want to hang out with this old man for a few hours?" Mathew told him it was a date, and his lordship looked at Lady Elizabeth. "You can come as well. I'm sure you will have plenty to add about the new library. And I think that Logan could use the help."

"He does fine on his own. I've never met a man who could convey so much with a simple quirking of his brow. I do believe you taught him that." They both laughed as Duncan sat a plate in front of Mathew. Lady Elizabeth continued as she took a chip from his plate. "You should also know that I've contacted a few of the faeries. They have agreed to come and see that the books that are shelved for you."

Duncan left the kitchen just as they were talking about the new wing that was being added to the library that would be for supernaturals only. It was going to have a special passage so that only they could enter. It would have information on their kind as well as an entire section on lineage.

Duncan made his way to the door when the doorbell rang. He was nearly there when Mel suddenly appeared and put her hand to his chest.

"No." He nodded, knowing that she of all people would know if it was safe for him to open the door. But when she started to reach for the doorknob herself, he was suddenly afraid for her. Duncan started to reach for his lordship when he and Lady Elizabeth were suddenly there. This could not be good.

~~~

Rythen stood very still. The woman who had appeared behind him made him slightly nervous, but he knew that she couldn't kill him. Hurt him like hell, but not kill. He turned slightly when he saw the man of the house in the doorway. But it was the woman behind him that had his full attention.

"I'll not harm anyone within." She nodded but didn't lower her sword from his throat. How she'd managed to sneak up behind him and draw it meant he had been resting for far too long. Rythen tried another approach. "I could kill you now and still take the household."

"You could try, but I'm betting you won't get very far with that either. See that man there?" He looked to his right where she was nodding. "That is the new king of Molavonta. You fuck with me and he'll bring a whole lot of hurt down on your ass. I'm Tess by the way. You should know my name when I run you through."

"New king? What happened to Sherman? And for the record, I thought him to be a spineless ass that needed to be taken out long before he became king." She didn't
~~~

move to acknowledge him. Rythen turned to the king. "You are a mate to Melody, I presume?"

"You would presume correctly. And just who the fuck are you to make me have to leave lunch with my daughter at her school." Before Rythen could answer, Elizabeth cleared her throat. She was as beautiful now as she'd been the day he'd given her life.

"I'm assuming he's here to see me. His name is Rythen, Maker of Magic. He is my…well, he's my sire." The young vampire made his way to the door. He supposed by this realm's standards he wasn't young but with all the beings around him, he was. Rythen put out his hand to meet him, but was shocked when the blade at his throat dug deeper.

"I've no desire to harm you, young Warrior Fae, but if you do not let me go, I will." She snorted, and he felt the blood trickle down his throat and was surprised by the pain that accompanied it. "You still wish to hurt me?"

She leaned to his ear, and Rythen had a moment of fear. "There is more power in that house than you can imagine. And not one of them are feeling all warm and fuzzy about you right now. Until one of them, or the king, says it's okay, I'm going to hold you this way until hell freezes over. Now behave and I won't put a hex on your dick."

He looked down at the appendage she'd threatened and wondered when it had become a target of pain for this realm. Rythen looked at Elizabeth as she moved forward. Finally someone would help him. Rythen did not want to cause a war by killing this fae. He just wanted to talk. And he realized at that moment that none of the beings around him knew his true meaning for being there today.

"Let him go, Tess, but please stick around. I don't know what the hell he wants but it can't bode well for us." Elizabeth stood near him as he was released. When he took a step toward her, she looked at him with so much hatred that he took a step back from it.

"My lady? Are you upset that I've come to see you?" Elizabeth nodded. "I assure you that it is only a visit and that—"

The youngest and the first human he'd ever seen stepped in front of Elizabeth, and Rythen took another step back. This little man was boiling with his hatred of him.

"You hurt my family and I will shoot you in the forehead and pee in your eyes." It might have been a funny threat if he wasn't so sure that the young man would do it. "You get out of here. I'm having lunch with my grandma and you're making everybody upset. Duncan is beside himself with worry that you'll call down the magic and hurt them all. And since I respect him a lot more than I do you, I don't want you here either."

"Grandmother?" Rythen looked at the king, who only shrugged. Then he looked at the vampire who was smiling at the human as if he were a proud parent. "I'm sorely confused. How could he be a grandson to any of you? He is merely a human."

Rythen felt his hair rise on his neck seconds before he was slammed against the wall of the house. The man who held him looked like he could take on the world and come out on top, and he had a powerful amount of magic running through him so that Rythen was impressed. Whoever had created him knew what magic really was. When he was slammed against the wall again, the man spoke.

"You touch my son and I will tear you to pieces and then let him pee on you. What the fuck are you doing here and why are you upsetting my family?" Rythen put his hand on the man's hand that held him at his throat.

"I've come to see Elizabeth. My name is Rythen, and I'm the creator of magic. The original magic. I have had a desire for some time to come to see her and how she is faring. I swear to you, I never meant to cause anyone any harm." When he was lowered to the floor but not let go, Rythen continued. "I am profoundly sorry that I've upset everyone. It was never my intentions. I'm confused, as you well might imagine, but I wish only to speak to my lady and see what wonders that this family has created on their own."

The man only looked at him, then took his hand away. Rythen could still feel his anger, but he only nodded. It was then that Rythen realized what he was.

"Good Christ. You're the Holder of Secrets." The man nodded, and Rythen bowed before him. "It is an honor to meet you, young man. I'm very…you are related to this family then?"

"My father-in-law owns this house." Rythen looked at the men still in the doorway, and the vampire stepped forward. "You've upset this family, sir, and for that you will apologize."

Rythen wanted to point out that he hadn't really done anything as yet, but turned to the family again. They were very protective of each other, and the young human in front of them was still looking at him like he would cause him great harm. Rythen leaned down to speak to him first.

"You are someone that I've never met before. A human, I mean. I've seen them…ones such as yourself…but never met one. What is your name?" The boy looked at his father, and Rythen waited. When the boy looked back at him, Rythen knew whatever came from his mouth was going to be great.

"With a person's name, there is power. You've given us yours, but I'm betting you only gave us a part of it. So I'll do the same to you. My name is Mathew. And when my grams tells me it's okay, you can have the rest." He leaned forward just a little and lowered his voice to continue. "You should also know that I've got my eyes on you. You mess up, I'm going to hurt you bad."

"Duly noted. As for my name, I will gladly share it with one as brave as you. I'm Rythen, Creator of all Magic. I have come to see your grandmother because it has been a very long while since I have seen her. Never in all my years away did I ever expect this sort of reception, and I am deeply sorry that I have upset all of them." The little boy stared at him for some time before speaking.

"I still don't really trust you, but I can see that you really are sorry. I can tell you who my family is, but not all of it. You'll have to earn that right." Rythen was impressed by the young man and put out his hand when Mathew did. "My name is Mathew Burris. And this is the house of Aaron."

Rythen stood up and reached for the vampire's hand. He'd heard about the man since he'd risen and was thoroughly impressed with everything that he'd heard. Before he could take his hand, however, the boy's father stepped between them.

"You still owe them that apology." Rythen nodded. He supposed in a way he did. He had come unannounced and had really upset everyone.

"I am profoundly sorry for this. I only meant to talk with Elizabeth and see how she is faring." He looked at the woman who had been his first and only creation other than magic. "I felt you, you see. Felt that you were…unhappy, and came to see what has happened."

Before he could say more, Elizabeth came to him. He could see the sadness in her eyes now. Whatever he'd felt, now that he was here, he could almost touch it, for it was that strong. She started to cry, his Elizabeth, and he felt something in him tear up as well. When she reached for him, he pulled her into his arms and simply held her.

"I know why you are here. But they do not. Please don't say anything until I've had a chance to prepare them." To say he was shocked by the news would have been an understatement, but to those around him and her, it was overwhelming. Especially the dapper man that only just then made an appearance.

"My lady?" She turned in his arms and looked at the man. "I have made you a sandwich of the finest beef and freshest vegetables. If you would come with me, I'll share another glass of sherry with you as well. All this nonsense about you being sad must be a mistake. Especially now when you have everything you ever wanted."

"I do have everything and more than I deserve. But I am…it is time that I do something else, don't you think?" When she turned to him, the queen Melody stepped forward. He watched her face when she, too, started to cry.

"Her mate, my grandfather, has gone to the fade, and now no one knows where he is. His flower, you see, it's died. And that could only mean one thing."

Rythen looked at them all before looking at Melody again.

"You believe that he has left the realm?" Melody nodded as her grandmother started to cry harder. "But he has not. He has been with me all these months."

"With you?" Rythen nodded at Elizabeth. "What the hell is he doing with you when I feel as if my heart has been torn from me? Tell him I want him here right now."

"I will, my lady, but I think he works on a project of great importance." He looked at the young human and wondered if this was the child he spoke of so often who would inherit so much. "You are the reason he works so hard, young Mathew Logan Burris. He works for you."

"Me?" Mathew looked at his father, then back at him. "On our project? He is putting it together?"

Rythen had a good deal more respect for the child now and knelt in front of him to see into his eyes. There was purity there as well as love for the man. And a good deal more that he'd bet that no one, not even the child, could see. He was brimming with untouched magic, magic that he'd bet his grandfather Aaron had given him in such small doses that no one had noticed.

"He is. He has…there have been some snags, you see, and he tends to forget about timeframes and such when he is working them out. He tells me that you've taken all of the pictures that accompany the book." Mathew nodded, and Aaron went to stand behind him.

"You are welcome in our home. But know that it is warded against magic that is used as ill intent." Rythen nodded and moved to cross the threshold, but was stopped by Melody. She was not as easy to convince as the rest.

"Bring my grandfather here." Before he could tell her he could not, she continued. "I don't care what he's told you. Can't you see what he's doing to my grandmother? I want her happy. Because when she's not, no one is. Bring him here."

Rythen snapped his fingers and held Elizabeth back when she went to go to her mate. He had taken her to Phillip rather than bring him out of his shell. There was no way she'd believe him if he told her what was really going on.

"He is working on this because he would like it finished before it is time." She turned to him. "You know as well as I do that the time for all is nearing. I have told you this day would come."

"And I have prepared for it as well as I could. I had forgotten, if you want me to be honest. Life had finally…it's been wonderfully blissful here and I simply forgot." She stared at her mate as she continued. "I don't have my things in order as you can well guess. I've been living, something I would imagine a man like you wouldn't understand. I know that my reign has come to an end. I guess in a way I knew that you'd be here soon, but I don't want to go. Not now that I know my love is alive."

"But you have no choice." She nodded and looked at him. "You will need to tell them. Soon too. They will need to prepare as much as you do."

"You think it will be that easy? That telling my family, whom I love more than I do anything in this realm or any other, that I'm going to die? You're off your noodle if you think that."

He had no idea what being off his noodle meant. But it didn't change the fact that he was there for one thing and one thing only…to end the creation he'd made to govern magick all those years ago.

CHAPTER 2

"I don't understand. What do you mean you're not ready? How could you be? I'm certainly not either." Elizabeth watched her daughter, Savannah, pace and wondered if she had taught that little annoyance to the family or they had taught her. Either way, she was going to miss it…that and so much more.

"You do too understand. It is as it was written. And as I have said to you countless times, I have come to the end of my time. I believe I have mentioned this to you before. But as usual you refuse to listen to what you do not want to hear." Elizabeth stretched out her legs in front of her and looked around her chamber. It was a mess of things she wanted to give away before the time came. "Do you want that large demi-god statue that was given to me by—?"

"I don't want you giving away your things anymore either. This is ridiculous. You're not going anywhere. And neither is Dad. I won't have it." Savannah sounded so much like Aaron at that moment that Elizabeth wanted to laugh. But she didn't. Savannah was upset with her, and she really didn't blame her.

"Look, love, I knew this day was coming. I'm not looking forward to it as much as I had before I knew where your father was, but it doesn't change the fact that it's going to happen one way or the other. It was written that I would end, and the time is growing near that I do. You should be happy to have me out of your hair." The intended joke did not go over as she'd planned, and Elizabeth got up to take her daughter into her arms. "I'm tired. More exhausted than I've ever been. And I've seen so much. Things that I could never tell you about that you'd believe."

"But I don't want to lose you. It was hard enough thinking that Dad was gone, and now this. I love you." Elizabeth felt her heart leap at the words like they did every time she said them to her. When she looked up at her, Elizabeth knew a moment of regret. But it would do her little good to have it. The contract was sealed.

"Your father is working so hard to make sure that Mathew has all he needs to finish the project that the two of them are working on. And when the time is right, you'll need to pass on what we've put together for him. He will need it." Elizabeth picked up the chain that held a small vial on it. "You'll see that he drinks it down?"

"You know I will. I would never want anything to happen to that little boy any more than you would." Elizabeth nodded and handed her the magic that would give Mathew the ability to live as long as he wanted and then some. He would also come into a power that would help him in the coming decades. Little Mathew was going to be a very powerful being when he turned twenty-five. They all made sure of that. Even Aaron.

She moved among her things as she thought of whom to receive her pretties, as she called them. There was so much of it that she'd had to, at one point, store it in a building that would hold it all. Even she had no idea what was there. But the things in this room were the things that meant the most to her.

"I should have done this years ago. I've so much stuff that…what on earth is that?" She picked up the long sheaf of paper and laughed. "I had wondered what happened to this. It's the original copy of the rules of magic. Your father was looking for these." Elizabeth put them with a few other things she was going to have Rythen take to Phillip. He would have to do what he wanted with them. "I wonder what other treasures I'll find."

"Mother?" Elizabeth turned to her daughter and saw the anguish on her face. "Don't let them take you from me. I need you both so much."

"It is for the best, Savannah. You'll see. Once I'm gone, any magic I have will come to you and Mel. She has a great deal, as do you, but you will have a bit of—"

"Please don't leave me." Elizabeth felt her heart break again. She'd only come here when the look on Duncan's face had hurt her when she'd looked at him. Elizabeth thought she'd miss him the most over her family. He and Aaron had been her best friends since she'd met them.

It was almost an hour later that Savannah took her leave. It was really good, too, because Elizabeth was close to breaking down and telling her that she had no desire to leave either. That she wanted her life to go on and on forever. But as she'd said to everyone countless times, it was as it was written. She would end her days in nineteen days, and there was nothing anyone could do about it.

Elizabeth remembered opening her eyes for the first time all those years ago. Rythen had been standing next to the table where she'd been laying, and he smiled at her. It was several days before she realized that the knowledge that she had in her head was something he'd given her rather than any experiences that she'd had. Even her knowledge of sex was something he'd implanted.

"You'll someday meet a man who will care for you a good deal more than I can. He will be your mate. Do you have it in your mind what that means?" She had nodded and smiled at him, and he asked her to repeat what she knew.

"It is a person who would love me no matter what, die for me if necessary, and put me above all else, including himself." Rythen nodded as she continued. "He will be my protector and my lover. He will guide me when I need it, distract me as well when it is necessary, and he'll stand beside me for all, even if he doesn't agree with me."

Elizabeth had thought he sounded boring and told Rythen that. "Be that as it may, he will be there for you. Sometimes, like my own life, I think it will be necessary to have something beside you for his or her help. It might have made me a better man had I found the time to create me a mate." He looked out the window where they sat. "You will find him to be the best thing that has happened to you and, at times, the worst. He will be a good mate to you."

"Will I know him?" She didn't know if she wanted a mate, but Rythen had told her it was necessary to have a friend when the time came. "What will become of me if I should not see him for what he is?"

"You'll know." Smiling at the thought, Elizabeth thought of the first time she'd seen Phillip. She had known what and who he was…it just took her a good deal longer to convince him.

Phillip sent her his love, and she basked in it. *"You old poop. The least you could have done was tell me you were alive. I've been thinking you never missed me at all."*

"But I did. You said that you had projects that needed seeing to, and I took that to mean you wanted to be left to do them." His love washed over her again. *"You really missed me?"*

"Not as much as I think I should have." He laughed, and she smiled. *"You know that I did. But please tell me that we'll be together soon. I want to spend some time with you before I go."*

"We go." She started to ask him what he meant, but he answered her first. *"I'll not spend a day without you where I cannot touch you and at least know that you are there for me when I return. You're my mate, and when you are gone, so shall I be."*

"There is no reason for you to – "

"There is every reason," he told her as he cut her off. *"I love you with all my heart and would not want to survive without you beside me. Where will I be without you? How will I want to breathe in and out if you are not there to scent up my air? You are my all, Elizabeth, and I would not have this any other way then to go with you in this as we have our life."*

Her heart ached to be with him, and she thought about him being with her. But when she spoke of it, she knew what he was going to say before he said it. He could not leave this project. Too many lives were at stake if he did.

"I shall see you soon, my heart." He told her that it wouldn't be much longer, and she knew that he was right in more ways than he knew. It wouldn't be long now. Just over two weeks. And she'd yet to tell her family the date was sooner than they'd thought.

~~~

Logan sat with Mac at the long table. He really liked the man and had learned a great deal from him in the few months that he'd been in this family. But now he was
~~~

trying to wrap his head around something that neither of them understood.

"You think that Rythen can be persuaded to change his mind?" Mac shook his head, and Logan had a feeling that he'd say that. "I don't want her to go. I love her like she was my own grandmother. I can't imagine what you and the rest of them are feeling."

"Like my heart has been ripped out." Mac opened his hand as he continued to speak, and a rolled parchment appeared there. "This is the contract that was signed all those centuries ago. Dad found it this morning and asked me to have you look it over. He said you might be able to find something with that vault of knowledge you now have."

It wasn't an unfair statement. He and Lizzy both had been given a great gift…or not…the day that they'd found the Book of Magic. Everything in it, and every other book on the shelves at the castle, was now, he supposed, downloaded into their minds. Logan had had Bradley, the alpha wolf, repeat it to him twice the day he'd told him what he'd found when he'd smelled him. Fucking bastard.

"Oh, and Bradley said to tell you that he's going to kick your ass. Did you really tell him that he was going to have eight more children?" When Logan nodded, Mac laughed harder. "Man, you should have seen the look on Aric's face when he told her. I thought she was going to kill him. But I have to know, is it true?"

"Yes. I cannot tell a lie." Mac shook his head and laughed again. "I just never told him that it would be because he would have two more sets of twins after this one. I thought it better that he think he was going to father five more separate births. More fun that way."

And more dangerous, he knew. The alpha was a great man, but he could hold a grudge like nobody he knew.

When Logan's phone rang, he stood up to take it. This was his work number, so he never knew what might come through it when he answered.

His secretary, Anna Peirce, had decided to retire some weeks ago. She'd told him that the hustle of him being mayor to a growing city was too much for her. So he'd given her a nice retirement package and sent her on her way. The new girl, Kim Craft, was working out okay.

"There is a man here to see you, and he's not very nice." Logan started to ask her who when she went on without his question. "He says his name is Ronald Jones and that he works for Rythen. You don't have an appoint…hang on a second."

He heard her fussing with someone and could only assume it was with Mr. Jones. When she told him to sit down and shut up or she'd kick his ass, Logan had a moment of worry. He had no idea who this man was, but could only assume it was someone with magic. As soon as Kim got on the line, he waited for her to finish her explanation before he could caution her.

"He said that he was to meet with you about a contract that needs to be signed off before things can progress. Something about you being the one to hold it. He won't tell me what it's about, nor the attorney who wrote it up. If you ask me, I think he's hiding something."

Logan would bet he was. Kim was human and hadn't been told what they all were as yet. He had wanted to make sure she was going to work out before he told her, and lately he'd not really had the time to mess with it. He had other things, like keeping his in-laws together, that were taking most of his time.

"Don't tell him where I am, and that if he doesn't make an appointment, I don't have time to see him." Logan looked at the contract that was still in Mac's hand. "Do me a favor, Kim…ask him if this has anything to do with Elizabeth."

When she came back to him after putting him on hold, she sounded like she was going to hit someone. He wished now that he'd worked at the office instead of coming home when he had. But Lizzy had said she was running late and that she'd not be there for Mathew when he got home from school. And since today was a big day in their family, he came home to be with him.

"He said that it is. He also said to tell you that time is of the essence and that he needs for you to sign your part of this before things could progress." He sat down with Mac and put the phone on speaker. "You're to sign off on this contract so that he can go back to his realm, whatever that means, and make sure that things are in the proper order before it is time."

"Time." He told her to have the man make an appointment and hung up. He looked at Mac. "If I'm understanding this right, I have to sign off on the contract to end your grandmother's days."

"Then you won't do it." Logan shook his head and smiled at Mac. "I don't think I like that look. It tells me that you're up to no good, and I'm pretty sure a few people are going to get pissed about it."

"Oh no. Not a few people but a particular man. I think that Rythen is going to be very pissed at me." Logan reached for Lizzy. He wanted her to see if what he thought was going on really was. Mac stood up to leave him and then turned.

"You should find out what the consequences are for either of you if you don't sign this. There might be things that will make it impossible for you not to sign it…such as someone will need to take her place." Logan nodded as Lizzy answered him.

"We're going to have a baby." The news was something that they'd both been anticipating for several days. And now it was official. *"I can't wait to tell them all. Dad is going to be so happy."*

Somehow Logan doubted that. The man had a real sore spot when it came to his daughter and sex. Logan wondered if maybe the man thought she was still a virgin, and knew that wasn't right. He knew the moment he'd made love to her in the elevator the first time he'd met her.

"I'm so glad. And you know that Mathew is going to be over the moon." At least he hoped so. The kid had been sort of moody for the past several days. *"Maybe he'll forget about Elizabeth leaving us, even if only for a little while."*

"I don't think so, but maybe. He really does love her and Grandda. They are almost as inseparable as Mathew and Dad. And those two spend a lot of time together." Logan smiled, knowing that Mathew was the buffer between the two of them. And when Aaron was told about the new baby, he'd make sure he was near his son. Aaron wouldn't harm him if he was in the same room. At least he hoped he wouldn't.

"When will you be home?" She told him in an hour. *"Good. How about I call your dad and see if he can take Mathew for a few hours. Then since Mathew won't be back from your parents' until six, we can celebrate being parents again. There is plenty of time for me to show you how much I love the fact that you're going to have my baby."*

"Sounds good. I'll try to get out of here earlier then. Oh, and Rythen was here. He said to tell you that not signing that contract won't help. He'll just go over your head. Do you know what he's talking about?" Logan shook his head. He should have known the man would have knowledge as to what he was thinking.

"Yeah, he said I had to sign off on your grandmother's ending paperwork. I was trying to figure out a way to make it so I didn't. Mac already told me that even if I didn't, there might be kickbacks." He picked up the copy of the contract and noticed the time and the date too as he looked at the first page. The date of it made his world rock. Logan got up to get a beer and noticed the calendar hanging on the fridge as he continued talking to Lizzy. *"Well shit. I'm going to read this thing over for your dad. Then I have a meeting with the city council in an hour, I just remembered too. How about a rain check for tonight?"*

"Deal. And I'll do you one better. I'll meet you at the courthouse for the meeting. I have a few things I'd like to bring up as well." Logan had to smile. He wanted to point out that she was a great deal like her dad again, but needed to look over his notes for the meeting. Lizzy was like her father in that she'd argue any point just so long as she was considered right. She was her daddy's little girl.

He left the house twenty minutes later. Time to make the city see what sort of man they'd brought in to make them a city again….and what sort of man they already had in place. He just hoped things went the way he thought they should.

CHAPTER 3

The woman sitting at the desk only looked at him when he shifted on his seat. Rythen had missed a great deal over the centuries, and the way women now dressed and acted was one of them. He wanted to ask her to walk to the large file cabinet again but was afraid she'd call him names again. Two of the ones she'd called him he was going to have to ask someone about. He had no idea what sexist meant but doubted it had anything to do with actual love making. But chauvinistic, that one baffled him the most.

"Mr. Rythen, Mr. Burris and the others will see you now." He stood up when she did and waited just long enough to have her walk in front of him. Yeah, he'd missed a great deal, and high heels were quickly becoming his favorite shoe.

As soon as she opened the door to allow him in, he moved into the room thinking he needed to find himself a nice little office with a nice secretary like the one out front. This woman worked for Aaron, so he knew she was aware of what they all were. As soon as he saw the three other women sitting around the room, he decided that he needed a large office with many women, all of them in the highest heels they could find. He wondered if they'd call him sexist too.

"Rythen, how are you?" Aaron showed him to a seat as he asked. "We've invited a few other people to this meeting. Some of them I think you might know."

He was introduced to all the men at the table and yes, he knew a few. He looked at Logan when he handed him his file. The man looked like he was very upset with him. Rythen didn't care. He knew that they'd all try to stop this thing with Elizabeth. But it would do little good. They had a contract.

"The reason for this meeting is to go over the outline of the plans for the city." Rythen opened the file to the first page thinking that this meeting would be boring. The only reason he'd come was because Aaron had told him he could meet him afterwards and if he didn't come, Aaron would see him some other time. This was not what he had in mind. The little boy, Mathew, stood up and sat down again in front of a computer. As pictures started to flash on the wall, Rythen found himself mesmerized by it all.

"The police station is the first thing we need to complete. As you know, most of the work on the new building is being funded by Black. The rest of the funding is to come through as donations from—"

"I've been thinking about that." Everyone turned to a man he'd been introduced to as Malian Tallis. "I believe that we should continue to use the Black monies to finish the project and start the one on the fire station immediately. The money that we've managed to raise, while not a lot, could start that one until the fire station is finished. It's been a hardship having to wait on the people to get up off their butts and donate like they should. But the money is right there. I think we should use it."

"That wasn't on the agenda. Malian, last month you were told if you want to add something constructive to the meeting it had to be brought to us forty-eight hours before we—" The man cut Logan off again.

"Yeah, yeah, you said that. And I only just thought of this. Why shouldn't we use what we can from the Black Corp? They said they'd help, and everyone here knows they have an endless supply of money." Malian winked at him as he leaned in to whisper. "Aaron here is said to be worth billions. Why not get a little for the town while he's still kicking?"

Rythen realized that the man had no idea that every being in the room could hear a pin drop and his whispered comment about Aaron could be heard by them all. Rythen looked at Aaron and was shocked to see that he was laughing. Did he really not hear him? Or was it that he cared little for the low opinion the man had of him?

"Black will only finance what was agreed upon." Logan took the file from Malian and opened it to the back pages before continuing. "As of right now there is less than ten grand in the account set up to make the necessary repairs on the buildings as well as the needed upgrades on the library. I'd like for you to explain where that money has gone. Nearly eleven million dollars of the money is missing. And if you interrupt me again, I will have you removed from this meeting."

"Now see here. You can't talk to me that way. I'm on the council, and as such I'm the voting majority for them. Do you see anyone else here that will stand up for this city? Not you, Burris. Last time I looked, you're not using any of that money you got from marrying into the family either." The low growl coming from Logan nearly made Rythen laugh. The human council member was going to be torn apart if he didn't shut up.

"And I have no plans of doing so. As for your comment about the council, I have it on good authority that you threatened the others about coming here tonight. You told Mr. Donley that if he showed you'd make sure that he was facing an audit of his department that would show him using the state funding for things other than research." Malian started to sputter, but Logan continued as if he were not. "Mrs. Sheppard said that you told her that her daughter's house would be foreclosed on, even though it's not in arrears. And that her son-in-law would lose his job with the city because you had that sort of power."

"Lies. I have no reason to threaten these people. They're just saying that because they think things are going to hell. And with you in charge, I can see it coming fast." A file slammed down on the table just as Malian started to rise. "What the hell is this?"

"Your own financial records." Aaron sat still as he continued. Nodding once to the little boy, pictures of Malian on a yacht with several younger women flashed on the screen. "I've got it on good authority that you're spending departmental money on your own little fun. How many times have you been to France this year, Malian? Twice? Three times?"

"I have a house there that I got from my wife's family." Another file was put in front of Malian. "You have no rights to dig into my life. What if I did a little digging into your life? What the hell would I find there?"

"I'm sure that you'd be surprised by what you found." Rythen nearly burst out laughing at Aaron. "But that's not the issue here. We're here to find out what you've been up to. And by the way, your wife was not happy to find these pictures. She is right now making sure that all your funding is cut off too. Along with a few other things."

Malian looked around the room, and Rythen could almost hear the man's mind working to figure this out. When the door behind him opened, Rythen stood up as Lizzy walked in. Behind her were three men dressed in suits. All of them looked to be armed.

"Hello, Malian my boy. You've been very naughty. It's a good thing my husband is in charge of this little parlay or you'd be in a great deal more shit than you already are. Oh, and I'm so glad you appointed me to the task force for the police. I bet you never thought…what did he call me, Mathew?"

"He said you were an airhead and that you didn't have as much brain power in one of your fingers as he did in his entire body." He grinned at his mother. "I guess he messed up your fingers with your brains."

Rythen was surprised by the information and was equally surprised that Logan had done nothing about it. Had it been his mate, he would have killed the man. But Malian stood up and when he did, the three men pulled their weapons.

"I said that in my office to my brother. There is no way you could have heard that." Mathew clicked on a couple of keys and an office with Malian and another man showed on the wall. The entire conversation about hiring Lizzy as their scapegoat was caught on record, and Rythen couldn't have been more impressed. He had missed a great deal more than he'd thought by being away.

The three men stepped forward and helped Malian to stand. "Malian Tallis, you're under arrest for embezzlement as well as fraud." Rythen watched as the man was dragged from the room screaming about his rights. Mathew stood to leave too, and Rythen stopped him.

"You helped them with this?" He nodded. "I'm very impressed. You were very helpful to them, and you made a very good case against him."

He wasn't sure what the boy was going to say. Mathew hesitated for a long while before he looked up at someone behind him. Rythen had a feeling it was his stepmother. When he looked back down at him, Rythen smiled.

"That's what family does. We help each other. And if you think I'm going to sit on my butt and watch you take away my grams just because you think you're all that, you're in for a big surprise. I'm not going to let you."

"There is no stopping what is happening, young man. Some things just are." Rythen turned to see Aaron behind him and stood up. "You should teach him that things don't always turn out the way you want them. There are laws."

"He knows about laws governing things more than I would bet you do. But what you don't understand is that he loves her. And that, my good man, will conquer all." Aaron put out his hand, and Mathew went to him. "Now, if you'll give me one minute, I'm going to say good-bye to my grandson. He has homework to do."

When the two of them left, Rythen sat down. This had to be the most stubborn family he'd ever encountered.

And over the years, he'd seen a lot of them…just not humans, and he wondered if they were all like this or if the people in this family were particularly stubborn. They were a different breed altogether, this house of Aaron. Rythen started to sit when the room tightened and he waited for whoever was entering the room to come. He was surprised to see Morriganna the witch.

~~~

Elizabeth moved along the passageway toward where she'd been told. She wanted to see…no, that wasn't right. She *needed* to see Phillip. Now. Right now. When she got to the door, she stopped, suddenly afraid. Morriganna had told her she'd only have an hour at best. This had to work. She wasn't sure that Morriganna could distract Rythen that long.

Opening the door, she nearly burst into tears when she saw him there. The fact that he knew was all she could think of, and as she moved toward him, she stripped off her clothing. When his shirt joined hers on the floor, she smiled.

"Are you sure about this?" He nodded at her and kicked his shoes across the room. "We're not really young anymore."

"No, and we won't get any older either if this doesn't work. Who came up with this anyway? I'd very much like to send them a thank-you note."

"Logan. And we can talk later. Right now, I want you." He pulled her now naked body to his and kissed her. The man knew passion and how to make hers rise to a nearly out of control fire in a very short amount of time. When he lifted his head, she pulled him to her again. There was no time to waste.
~~~

When he dropped to his knees in front of her, she nearly got down as well. But when he pulled her body to his mouth, Elizabeth nearly cried out. Never had he done anything like this before.

He ate at her over and over until she was weak with it. Her first climax nearly had her tumble over on top of him, and the second and third had her trembling. Begging him to stop only made him work harder until she finally had to pull him from her.

"You're killing me." He grinned at her and leaned in to suckle at her clit again. The short yet powerful release had her whimper. When he stood up, she had to hold onto him.

"I'm going to enjoy this. As many times as I can." Phillip backed her up until she felt the table behind her touch her back. He lifted her up and sat her on the table and moved between her thighs. His cock slowly entered her until she thought she'd die from the pleasure.

"Phillip, I love you." He moved to her breast and suckled on the tip before pulling the heavy flesh into his mouth. His tongue moved over the nipple over and over as he entered her deeper and then deeper still. When he was as deep as he could go, he looked at her.

"You're so hot, my love. And wet. You've been thinking of this, haven't you?" He rolled his hips, and she could swear he was at the back of her throat. "Come for me. Tighten that pretty pussy around me and come."

Phillip had never talked to her this way before. They'd been together for so long that she rarely thought of sex anymore. But this man, this man who had been away from her for so long was making her think of things she'd never thought of before.

"I want to take you into my mouth." He groaned and rolled his hips again. "I want to taste you too. Feel you fucking my mouth."

"You're going to make me come too soon if you keep that up." Elizabeth rolled her own hips and watched his face. His fingers on her hips tightened, and she knew that he was close.

Wrapping her ankles around him, she sat up and took his mouth. His body started to move in and out of her faster now, and she felt her climax rolling along her body. When he nipped at her throat, Elizabeth threw back her head and cried out at her release. His body exploded in hers even as she felt his mouth bite down hard enough to draw blood. Her next climax had her seeing stars. His own roar of completion made her feel like she could take on the world. Holding onto him, she felt her love for him warm her entire body.

"I know you have to go back soon, but I just need to hold you for a bit longer." Elizabeth nodded, unable to speak at the moment. "I love you, dear. And always will. And I've missed you."

"I've missed you too. When Logan saw that we could become human if we had a child to raise, I nearly leapt with joy. A child was all I could think of. We should have thought of this sooner, having more children." He nodded against her throat and she continued. "Morriganna said that we'd have a chance right now but we'd have to be careful. Rythen will not like being thwarted."

"He won't. I didn't even consider what he was doing when he asked me to finish this book without interruptions. To have me locked in here…I didn't even try to leave until Logan contacted me. He said that it is in the contract that only you can be taken from this world."

He lifted her up and sat in a chair with her in his lap. "I won't live without you. You're my life, and I can't stand the thought of living it without you by my side."

"I know. I had thought of his coming to me a few years ago, but dismissed it as it being too far away to think about. Then when Mathew was talking about how he'd been reading some of the older books in Aaron's library, I thought of our own and decided to share some with him. I pulled down several books when the contract fell on the floor in front of me." She laid her head on his shoulder as she continued. "Phillip, if this doesn't work and we can't have a child, I want—"

"Don't, love. Please. I love you and don't want to think about that right now." He put his hand over her flat belly and smiled. "I remember feeling our own Mathew growing here for the first time. He was such a good baby. I miss him daily."

It had been over one hundred and fifty years since he'd died. Mathew had gotten something that had made him ill from earth and had died a few weeks later. There had been a human woman, Dawn, that had given birth to his child, and she'd never told anyone. It was only by chance that they'd found Sara and had brought her to the family.

"Do you suppose we'll survive the human world?" His humor made her smile. "There are things there that frankly scare the pants off me."

She shifted on his nakedness and grinned at him when he moaned. "You seem to have a handle on it right now. I think we should make sure we did it right once more before I go."

He turned her on his lap and lifted her up. When Phillip lowered her onto his cock, she looked at him, surprised. This was something he'd never done either. When his fingers gripped her hips, pulling her forward and back, she got the hang of it and started to ride him. Every time her clit touched his pelvis, she felt her center start to build again.

"Phillip, please, I need to come again." He slid his fingers down her body to her pussy and pressed his thumb against her every time she rolled forward. As soon as she came again, he pulled her tight against him and took her mouth. When she cried out again, coming hard against him, she felt his cum fill her again. She wondered if she'd ever be able to move after this. Closing her eyes, she laid on his shoulder as tremor after tremor took her. When she settled finally, he lifted her chin up with his fingers.

"It's time." Nodding, she stood up and reached for her clothes. Tears threatened to overflow from her eyes, and she tried hard to not let them go. She didn't want their last few minutes together after what they'd just shared to be sad. When he said her name, she turned and looked at him.

"I've made this for you to give to Mel. It's memories of all our lives together. Even if we can make it out of this, we might not have those, and I'd very much like for someone to have them." Taking them, she put the thick book to her heart and held it there. When he kissed her good-bye, she turned to leave. Turning at the door, she looked at him.

"I love you with all my heart." He nodded. "I will never forget you. Ever. If this doesn't work, you'll be the last person I think of and will forevermore be in my heart."

Elizabeth left him before he could speak. Her heart was breaking, and she thought he knew it. Finding the way back nearly got her lost twice, but finally she was at the opening, where the Fates were waiting.

"Don't tell me. I already know." They all nodded. "There was no child conceived today. But we all knew it was a long shot. I even think Phillip knows."

"He does. I'm so sorry, my lady. I had hoped that…." Lachesis turned away from her before finishing. "He is a good man, your mate. I wish that I had news that I could share with you."

So did Elizabeth. But she knew that asking them anything would get her nowhere. They had their secrets just as she did. And moving along the corridor to the outside, she took a deep breath before turning to them.

"Can you at least tell me if he dies with me?" None of them would look at her, and she turned back to her walking. "I swear there are times when I want to smack you all. I wonder if there will ever be a time when I get a straight answer from you."

"No. And if you did, you'd not believe us." Atropos walked beside her as her sisters moved back. "There is something I can tell you. Things are not as bad as they seem. Your granddaughter, Lizzy, she is with child. Did you know that she will have a great leader someday? And that she will rule the vampires with her mate until all is well with them?"

"Yes. You told me that before." Elizabeth turned to look at her when she stopped walking. "You want to tell me something, but I have a feeling that you're going to make me work for it."

"I will." Elizabeth would have gladly zapped her but was afraid she'd only harm herself. "And you would be correct. You don't want to harm me, Elizabeth the queen. You want things from me that you know that I cannot give you. But there are some things…things that will need your help to come to fruition."

"Such as?" Clotho walked up to her and took her hand. "You're going to take me now?"

"What a thing to ask. I do not want you gone at all. Now pay attention. I can only say this to you one time. You will have all you want if you give him what he least expects." Elizabeth waited for more but nothing was forthcoming. "Understand?"

"No." Elizabeth wanted to stomp her foot. "Do you have any idea how many men I know that want something that they least expect? I don't suppose you could give me a hint as to who this might be?"

"You know." Elizabeth growled at Lachesis. "You do that as well as Aaron the king of Vamps. I wonder if he taught you."

Elizabeth started walking again. Her time was running short and she was so frustrated right now that if she started to argue with the Sisters Three she'd be there for centuries. Or at least until her time was up. Was it really only twelve more days?

She was back in her chamber when she let go of her tears. It was going to end this way, and the sooner she got used to the idea the better. Going to her bed, she decided that a nap was in order and closed her eyes. But all she saw behind her lids was the family she was going to miss more than anything. It was time to tell them good-bye.

CHAPTER 4

Rythen sat in the chair for a long time after his meeting with Logan. The man refused to sign off on this. Not that he blamed him, but he needed to have his signature on this or things would have to go a different route. Who would have thought that a powerful queen such as Elizabeth had been would have so many people so loyal to her. Not even the beings at the castle had a bad thing to say about her, and apparently Mel, the current queen, was just as wonderful.

"No one can be that good. I never meant for her to be thought of this way." He looked around when Aaron cleared his throat. "I'm thinking aloud. Is that not something that is done here?"

"Sure it is," he told him. "But usually he does it when there isn't a room full of people. What's eating at you?"

And that was another thing. The sayings. Nothing was eating at him, and he felt the overwhelming urge to produce something and have it chew on his leg for a bit. But he doubted that anyone would see the humor in it. No one here seemed to like him overly much.

"I'm upset that I cannot get young Logan to do what I need for him to do. And then there is the added fact that I don't understand this world at all. You had that man arrested. He was skimming money. I have no idea what that term means."

Aaron sat down across from him and smiled. He had several smiles, Rythen noticed, and each of them had a different meaning. This one, Rythen thought, said "you're not a very bright man so I'll explain things to you so you can understand." Rythen thought that this one irritated him the most.

"I can have my grandson get you a copy of the urban dictionary. Some of the things we say have a great many definitions and a few that are off the wall funny." Rythen doubted it would help and told him so. "Your loss then. Why is it important that Logan sign off on the contract?"

That was another thing he didn't like…the rapid change of subject. Could these people not wait until one conversation was finished before starting another? Apparently not. Rythen looked at the men in the room still there and wondered how such a group of men, most of them older by far than Logan, could get along so well.

"He is the Keeper of Secrets. And as such he cannot tell anyone what the contract says." He looked at Aaron when he didn't say anything. "It is his job to do such, yet he tells me no as if he has a choice."

"He does. Elizabeth and Phillip granted him and my daughter that title, and with it they gave him free will. With that, they can tell you to fuck off or not." Rythen had been told to fuck off too. Several times just today. Aaron laughed as he continued. "I love my new son-in-law, and more so because he's shit in your oatmeal so soundly."

Rythen didn't even ask. What would be the point? Aaron would make fun of him and he'd be upset more than he was now. Rythen thought of another tactic to get the younger man to sign off. But before he could think it through, Sara moved into the room as silent as a breath.

"You do and I will tear you apart." Aaron stood up and took his wife into his arms. Rythen wanted to believe it was because he loved her, but he had a feeling he was saving his life.

"I was only thinking it. I would never have…." She glared at him, and Rythen flushed. "It would work. I would only hold them captive until he put his name on the lines where I need them. The young man would think it an adventure."

"You'll still be in a world of hurt." Aaron watched him as Sara continued. "He thought to take them hostage until Logan did as he wants. And his idea of hostage would be holding them apart and telling them that the other was dead. He is no longer welcome in our home."

"You would have done that?" Rythen shook his head, then nodded at Aaron. "You worthless piece of shit. I should run you through for such a thought. To think that you would make them suffer to get what you want. What sort of man are you?"

"A being that is used to getting what he wants." Rythen stood up. "I'm going to the castle. You people are not what I expected when I came here. I thought you'd be well and truly ready to get rid of her. She was supposed to keep everyone in line, not be their friend."

"And that makes her a bad person in your eyes?" Rythen looked back at the man he'd been introduced to. Bradley Wolff, alpha and leader of the largest pack of wolves in the world, stood waiting for him to answer.

"I've seen what a person who has no authority can do to a realm. She has let things slide." He flushed when Aaron snorted at him. There had been nothing showing that she'd been anything but an outstanding ruler, and her children were just like her. "You've no idea what will happen when there is no one to stand up to the bad as well as the good."

"Ah. So you think you have the market cornered on seeing what happens when rulers don't do their job. I see. And how is it that I run such a successful pack? Do you suppose it's because I kill all that go against me? I wouldn't have much of a following if I did that. Or do you think that I too, rule my people with a light hand?" Bradley sat down, but it didn't look to Rythen as if he were relaxed. He looked more poised to leap as he waited for an answer.

"I don't know what you're talking about." But he did, and he was sure the wolf knew it. "I'm talking about the kingdom of Molavonta and all the magic within." Bradley nodded and smiled. "You don't expect me to believe that you care to compare that world with your own?"

"I do. And you should know that as a leader, I have taken my cues from the people I respect. And one of them is Elizabeth. What do you suppose would have happened had she been a harsh ruler as you think she should be? Do you think that her having so many loyal friends, that they would have come to her defense? And if you think that Logan is giving you no help, don't even come to my pack house again. There will be no one there to save your ass this time."

Rythen wanted to rub his leg where there had been long bites taken from him. The female alpha, Aric, had told him that he'd be better off leaving on his own, but he'd tried to reason with her to get Logan's help. The sixteen or so shifters that had been there had attacked him within seconds of him demanding that she see him. He was sure the only thing that had kept them from hurting him more was her shrill whistle. Rythen left by way of magic before they could attack again.

Rythen left the office in favor of his chamber at the castle. But as soon as he entered, a guard was stationed at his doorway. He reached for Mel to ask her why he was being held prisoner.

"You're not. I'm putting my men there to keep you safe. As of right now there are a great many of my subjects that would enter that room and try to murder you. And believe it or not, it was hard for me to find guards that would watch over you. Imagine that."

He felt a surge of anger wash over him. Rythen wanted to scream at her that this was her fault, but he knew that he was the one doing this. They all loved his creation, but it was out of his hands. The contract was to be fulfilled or he'd look the fool.

Rythen paced his bedchamber for an hour before he finally sat down. In eleven days now he was going to have to end the life of someone that had meant—and still meant—the world to him. He actually thought about doing it sooner but knew that if he tried, he'd be signing away any privileges that he had now. Few that they were.

He was going to have to figure out a way to make these people see reason. Perhaps he should talk to Aaron again. The man had been around for the longest, and he would see reason…at least Rythen hoped he would. But maybe not after he found out what he'd been thinking about his grandson.

~~~

Kim was coming back from her break when she saw the man. He'd been there before, but this time she had a feeling he was lost rather than looking for someone. She
~~~

walked up behind him and touched his shoulder. He turned so quickly that she nearly fell over. But he caught her before she could fall. It was the first time she'd been close enough to smell him. And boy oh boy did he smell good.

Being held in his arms was amazing too. She wasn't sure what she had expected from a man this tall, but he was looking down at her with such intensity that she felt herself flush. He even cupped her closer to him when she started to move back.

"Mr. Rythen, perhaps you should let me go." He nodded but didn't move. When she started to push him back, she felt his cock as it thickened on her thigh.

"You're very lovely." Nodding, she pushed a little harder on his chest and found the hard muscles there almost too good to be true. "I would very much like to kiss you."

"I don't think that's such a good idea. I have a boyfriend and he gets very jealous of me being touched by other men." Mr. Rythen nodded but still held her. "You really need to let me go."

"Please, just a small kiss." Before she could tell him no again, his mouth brushed over hers in the most gentle of touches. And when he did it again, it was all Kim could do not to run her fingers into his hair and pull him back. As he lowered his head to hers a third time, she had a moment to think about what the others had said about him being something of an oddity, and wondered if she was going to get fired over this. Then his mouth took hers.

There was no simple kiss in the way his mouth moved over hers. He didn't just kiss her so much as taste her and take everything she had. When his tongue moved over her lips, she felt as if she had no choice but to allow him entrance, and moaned when his heat entered her mouth. Kim decided that her boyfriend could go to hell; this was what a real man felt like. When something hard touched her, she moaned again when he rocked his hard shaft into her pussy.

"You're not supposed to be here." She nodded, not having a clue what he was talking about. "I've waited centuries for you, and now that you're here, you're not what I can have."

"I want you to take me." She nearly cried out when he lifted his head from her throat, and whimpered when he rocked into her again and again. "Please, you're making me ache doing this. Just take me."

"Oh, I would love to, but someone is coming down the hall." He pulled back from her and held her until she was steady. "You're very delicious. What I wouldn't give to take you back to my chambers and ravish every inch of you."

It was on the tip of her tongue to tell him to do it, but she saw her boss at his door. She wondered how much he'd seen. When Mr. Rythen turned, she realized that Logan had seen a great deal, and he was not happy about it.

"So, you've decided to seduce my help in order to get what you want?" For some reason that hurt her more than she could say. Moving away from both men, she made her way to the bathroom to repair the damage she was sure Mr. Rythen had done to her. Looking in the mirror, Kim was shocked to see just how much he'd mussed her up.

Not only was her hair mussed up, her blouse was pulled from her skirt and her buttons on the top were undone. He'd done that while he'd been kissing her? Trying to straighten her clothing, she nearly screamed when someone came out of the stalls. The beautiful woman there merely smiled at her as she washed her hands.

"You're the one. The one I'm to give him that he doesn't know he needs." Kim shook her head, not really sure what Ms. Elizabeth was talking about as she continued. "He kissed you and nearly made love to you in a matter of seconds. Has that ever happened to you before?"

"No, and it won't again. He…I don't know what happened out there, but…how did you know?" Kim felt her body heat again at the thought of what the two of them had nearly done and shivered. "Never mind. I don't care. I have a boyfriend and he's going to ask me to marry him soon. And when he does, all the other things going on with him will stop."

He'd told her that he was stressed with not having a job. And her mistake last night had been to point out that he'd not been looking very hard for one. His fist had come out so quickly that she'd had no time to dodge it. He'd hit her in the side of the head so hard that she'd seen stars. Next time, she told herself, she'd learn to keep her mouth shut.

"You think that will solve things? You keep your mouth shut a great deal, my dear, yet he still uses you as a punching bag. And if you marry him, you think it will make things better between the two of you?" Ms. Elizabeth put her hand near where Josh had hit her, and the pain seemed to dissipate instantly. "It will only get worse if you stay with him. And I think you know it."

Shaking her head, Kim felt the tears as they filled her eyes. This woman didn't know what she was talking about. There was no way she was going to marry a man like her father had been. Looking in the mirror once more, she decided that she'd done all she could about her appearance. Moving to the door, she stopped when Ms. Elizabeth said her name softly.

"He'll kill you if you stay, Kim Craft. This I will promise you. Mark my words. If you continue to think that he loves you and that when he hits you it is somehow your fault, he will kill you because you have allowed him to." Kim didn't bother answering her but went out.

Josh Gibson, her abuser and the man she lived with, had told her the day before yesterday when she'd left for work that he was going job hunting. And when she'd returned from work with her first paycheck, he was still in the same clothes that he'd had on before she'd left. A pair of pants that hung well under his bulging belly, dirty tee shirt, and a pair of socks that looked as if they would stand on their own if he ever took them off. Trying her best to figure out how to word asking him if he'd had any luck without upsetting him, he'd told her that he'd remembered that today was payday for her and wanted to see her first check. But she'd lied to him.

"It's not here yet. And I'm not sure, but I think I have to set up a direct deposit in order to get my checks." He'd been visibly angry about that and she'd backed away from him. "I can't help what the rules are, Josh, I can only follow them so I can keep the job."

He'd punched the wall to the side of her head and walked away. The hole there had been a nasty reminder for the rest of the night of what she should and shouldn't do to upset him. That's when she decided that she'd better open a checking account, and she thought she might not put his name on it. But he'd given her the papers this morning for her to sign off on to allow him access to the account. Kim still had them in her purse. She still wondered how he'd managed to get them.

When she was sitting at her desk again, she nearly leapt up when the door behind her opened. Mr. Rythen looked at her before he walked past her without a word. Logan asked to see her in his office. This was it; she was going to lose her job.

She was surprised to see Ms. Elizabeth there, along with Lizzy. The two of them looked like they'd been handed the worst sort of news. Kim felt the need to comfort them even though she was sure she was not going to be employed in a few minutes.

"I'd like to have you come over to my house tomorrow. I have some work that would require you to stay on for a few days. I'd pay you for all your time, of course, and you'd—"

"I thought you were going to fire me." She flushed when she cut Logan off. "I'm sorry. I don't make it a habit of kissing your clients. I'm not even sure what came over me. He startled me and I fell. When he tried to save me from falling on my ass, I guess he thought I was offering myself to him. I wasn't, but I can see how he would have thought so. I'm not usually so clumsy, but he was so lost looking that I wanted—" She stopped talking when Lizzy laughed. "I'm sorry. I go on about nothing when I'm scared."

"Do I frighten you, Kim? Do any of us?" Kim looked at Logan and the two women. "Because I have to tell you that I hope not. We've come to enjoy having you work for us. So much so that we decided to come clean with you."

"No. You don't. I've just been going through something personal, and I tend to…are you going to fire me?" He shook his head. "Why not?"

"Do you want me to?" Kim said no. "Good. But there are some things that I think you should know about us before you continue working for me. There are things, like us for instance, that will make you think you've gone off the deep end. But it's time you were told. And first of all, I don't want you to leave, so I've taken the liberty of pinning you to the chair. All right?"

She tried to move and when she couldn't, she started to panic. Josh had tied her up once to prove he was her boss and she'd never gotten over the feeling. When Lizzy was suddenly in front of her, she looked into her eyes as she commanded her to do.

"Take deep breaths. That's it, long and slow in and slower out." She did as she asked. "Logan has freed you from the bonds, but you're still terrified. Was it the boyfriend who did this to you? Or someone else."

"Josh. He said that he was my superior and when I begged him to let me go, even going so far as to argue with him, he beat me until I lost consciousness. While I was out, he tied me to the bed and raped me." Kim tried to close her mouth, but it was as if she had no will power over not telling Lizzy the truth. "Please don't tell him I said anything. It will upset him terribly."

"I won't. But Grams is right, he will kill you if you stay with him. And you're better than that." Kim didn't think anything of the kind and told her so. "I think I can prove it to you if you'll let me."

"Why?" Lizzy frowned at her when she asked, and Kim decided that she was a fool. "Why do you care whether or not he kills me? Not even my own family cares that much."

"We're not that kind of family. And for the record, your family sucks." Kim laughed at Logan. "I'd like to tell you what we are. Are you okay to handle that?"

Nodding, she wasn't so sure. Kim had a feeling that once she knew this, nothing was ever going to be the same in her little world again.

"I'm a vampire, a day walker, and Lizzy is one as well. But we have a good deal more than just the power that comes with that; we're both the Keeper of Secrets. We know all there is to know about each species, as well as a few humans."

"Day walkers." He nodded at her, and she looked at Ms. Elizabeth. "And what are you? The queen of all vampires, and you're going to change me into what they are so I can be your sexual slave?"

"Good heavens. Where do you young people get this stuff?" Elizabeth sat beside her. "No, dear. While I was queen, it was of magic, not vampire. Though I did help govern them as well. My granddaughter is queen now. You've met her, Melody."

Kim felt her world start to tilt, and when she stood up, she had to close her eyes against the way the floor moved beneath her feet. Hearing her name being shouted didn't keep her from falling. Only it wasn't the floor she landed on, but into the arms of Mr. Rythen. How the hell did that happen?

CHAPTER 5

Rythen was pissed. The girl had no idea what was going on, and now these people were telling him he'd either mate with her or she'd have to be removed from his room. There was no way that these…beings could tell him what to do. He was older than the lot of them. When a small noise sounded from his bed, he stopped moving and looked at her.

He couldn't believe that someone had figured out this quickly what she was to him. All he'd done was kiss her once, and now it was as if he'd had a crier running from town to town with the information, telling everyone. The girl was human after all. What was he supposed to do about that?

"Where am I?" Her voice reached across the room to him like a caress, and he wanted to go to her and hold her. "I was at work having…I was dreaming."

"No, you weren't." She started to stand, and he went to her. It was hard for him not to lay her back on his bed and kiss her again, but there was not going to be any more of that. He was here for a job, not to find himself shackled to a human.

"What do you mean, no I wasn't? I wasn't at work, or I wasn't dreaming?" Rythen touched her face with his fingers because he felt as if he had no choice. When his fingers felt scorched by her heat, Rythen leaned in and brushed his mouth over the same area. Her fingers laced around his arms.

"You're very beautiful." Encouraged that she didn't push him away, he leaned into her throat and licked her pounding pulse. "I would like nothing more than to taste you right now. Sink my teeth into your creamy flesh before taking you on this bed. My cock aches to be buried deep inside of you where I know that I will find my only completion."

"Please." Rythen cupped her ass and brought her to his cock, and moaned. Even with her clothing on he could feel her heat. All of her. But there was no way he could do this. Not with this girl. Lifting his head, he looked into her lust-glazed eyes and felt his body tighten all the more.

"You're going to have to forget this. There is no way this is going to happen. I'm sure that Logan and the others told you to seduce me into this, but it won't work. I've no need for a woman such as you." He felt her stiffen and knew that he'd had it right. "They just want me to mate with you so that you can persuade me not to kill Elizabeth."

"A woman like me? And just what sort of woman do you think I am?" He didn't get a chance to answer her when she slapped him across the mouth. His head snapped back so quickly that he felt his neck pop. She was moving toward the door when he caught up with her. And that was a mistake he promised himself he'd never make again.

She was like a wild animal. Her nails raked over his face several times before he could hold her down. Then her feet scraped along his legs so hard that he was sure she'd hit bone. Every time he thought he had control of her, she used some other part of herself to get at him. Finally, he'd had enough and told her to stop.

"What is wrong with you? No woman would dare touch me in the way you have. If I had a good mind, I'd kill you right now." Not true. Firstly, he could never harm her; and secondly, he was quite proud of the fact that she thought she could win against him. When she moved toward the door again, he told her to stop, but she only continued as if he'd said nothing. When she crossed the threshold, he went after her. He was not finished talking to her as yet.

What happened next still baffled him. He'd been going after her to bring her to heel, and the next thing he knew he was laying on the floor with a large dragon on his back. And he was holding him in a way that Rythen could not use his magic on him. The girl was being held in the arms of Savannah and sobbing. He wanted to point out that he was the one being held down.

"What is the matter with you?" Draco, he thought is name was, asked. "Are you without any kind of sense? Did you think that harming one such as her would not get you imprisoned?" Rythen felt Draco's foot press him harder into the floor. "I will hold you here until we are at the bottom of this."

"This is Logan's fault. He told her to have sex with me, then have her keep me from fulfilling my duty to this kingdom." Saying it aloud sounded almost like he was insane. Trying again, he was cut off when the girl stepped forward.

"You think Logan would want me to…are you even hearing yourself? Why the hell would he care that…Christ, are you a dragon?" Laughter rumbled from

Draco as he assured her that he was. "I'm still dreaming, aren't I?"

"No, my lady, you are not. You're in a magical kingdom and I am a dragon. Would you like it better if I were to shift to human? This idiot would be able to get up, but I would not have you frightened of me." She shook her head. "Good. It is my understanding that Logan and his lovely mate were telling you what they were. Nice couple they are. Have you met Mathew? He and I are working together on a project. He is very smart."

"Draco, you're scaring her again." Savannah looked at Rythen. "If I allow you up, will you behave yourself?"

"I did nothing wrong. But if you would be so kind as to have this large foot off me, I'd be ever so grateful." Rythen looked at the women and wanted to say something, but he had no idea what. Just as the foot was lifted off his back, he decided that he had better come up with something or the dragon would have him for his supper. He would hate to have to spend the rest of his days in the belly of a large, bad tempered dragon.

When he was standing again, Rythen started toward her, only to come up short when Savannah put up her hand. He more than likely could have broken her barrier, but the truth of the matter was he was sort of afraid that he couldn't. Melody entered the room just as he was contemplating trying.

"You're making enough racket to wake the dead. You've brought a human to my realm to do who knows what, and Draco tells me that you're telling stories about Logan and the rest of my family. What do you plan next, Rythen? Do you plan to storm the castle and take it over? I assure you that you will not win in this."

There were several things he could have said to her, one of which was that her family was really his as well as he had created the sire to them all. Secondly, he had not told a lie. He, like the queen, was incapable of lying. And lastly…he looked at the girl again.

"She was told to seduce me." Melody looked at the woman. "And I've no idea what her name is. Either tell me so I can refer to her as something more than *the woman,* or that will be her name."

"You're an idiot." The woman started toward him again, but he stood his ground. There was no way he was backing down from her so that others could see. "My name is none of your business, you cynical over blown piece of fucking shit."

Rythen might have been impressed had he any idea what she was talking about. He got the namecalling, just not why she felt the need to say them to him. Just as he opened his mouth to tell her she was wrong, Shamus was in front of him.

"You'll do well to listen with your ears and not your heart right now, Rythen. While I'm not as old as you, I do know that a woman's scorn can and will harm worse than a sword." Rythen looked at the three women and thought maybe in this the new king was smarter. With a short nod, Shamus stepped back and nodded to the woman.

"Her name? May I please have her name?" He looked at Shamus and then Melody. "Do any of you know who she is?"

"Maybe they're waiting for you to ask me what it is, you nimrod. And again, I'll tell you that it's none of your business. What right did you have to do those things to me? Kissing me like I was…like you owned me." Rythen opened his mouth to remind her that she had enjoyed it as much as he, but he glanced at Shamus to see him shake his head. "And another thing, I have someone who loves me. He doesn't treat me right, but he says that he loves me."

"Who? Who is this man who dares to claim what is mine?" As soon as the words left his mouth, he knew that he'd made a major mistake. And if the look on either Shamus's or Melody's face was any indication, he was not leaving there without explaining himself.

"She's your mate?" Rythen didn't bother answering Savannah, but looked at Shamus. Surely, as another man, he'd help him.

"You have brought your mate here, in my castle, without telling her what she is to you? You've tried to claim another man's mate?" Melody started pacing and turned to look at him as she continued. "You'll make this right or so help me there will never be another ring for you to hide in so long as there is breath in my body."

"You would deny me space in my own creation?" Rythen moved toward her and was only a step closer when a blade was at his throat. The guard had come from nowhere and the Warrior Tess was right in the front of them. He was getting mightily sick of this woman and her troupe.

"You move—I mean so much as an eye lash—and I will cut your, what you think of as an impressive, dick off and give it to the faeries. I'm sure that they can use it as fertilizer for a plant or two." He felt his face flush at her words. No one spoke to him that way. Just as the sword bit just a little deeper into his skin, he decided that he'd stay in one piece if he simply spoke calmly.

"Logan and his father-in-law have rigged it so that I think her my mate. There is no way, after all this time, that mine should show up at just this time in my life." He felt the blade ease, but it never left his throat. "I've no desire to have a mate now, and having one as a human is just not feasible. I've no time to train her on the way that I run things."

"You think you'll need to train her…never mind that. I don't think I want to hear what lame excuse you might have for what you see as training. So you think that Aaron has…what did you call it? Oh yes, Aaron had made you think that K…that the woman is your mate when you know better? I see. And if I told you that it's impossible for that to happen, you'd not believe me either?" He nodded at Melody, who shook her head. "I cannot lie any more than you can. But listen to me. It. Can. Not. Happen. But you don't need to take my word for it. Let me call in the Fates."

Before he could tell her that wouldn't be necessary, the Sisters Three were standing in the room. Each of them hugged and kissed the others in the room, including Draco, before turning to him. Rythen had never been able to control these women, and was sure that now would be no different.

"You should know that as for now, I'm keeping Logan from you. He would like nothing better than to come here and rip you apart. I don't believe I've seen him so upset before." Clotho sat down on a chair that appeared behind her just as she needed it. "Come here, my dear, and sit with us."

"I'd like to go home now, please. I'm sure that Josh is worried about me." So the man who would dare touch what was his was Josh. If he could only find her name, he'd be set. The woman moved toward the door, and Rythen growled. "Is he going to hurt me?"

"Oh no, love. He can't. But Josh will if you leave now. There are things going on at your apartment that would make you be safer here." Atropos patted the seat next to her as a couch took the place of the large chair. "You come and sit with me. I'm sure you have a great many questions, and we're in the mood to answer them. Aren't we, sisters?"

Lachesis smiled and Clotho got up to get the woman. Rythen watched as the four of them got cozy on the furniture with the woman between them. Clotho looked at him and smiled.

"We've no use for you at the moment, Rythen. Be gone." When he felt the air rush around him, he knew that wherever he ended up he was not going to be happy about it. As soon as he looked around at Aaron and Logan, he wanted to scream. He had gone from the den to the frying pan in a heartbeat.

~~~

Elizabeth sat very quietly and listened to Logan tell Rythen what was going on. There was no way that the man could seriously believe that any of them would play such a cruel trick on him. But then she thought of what he'd done by making sure that she and Phillip were apart when they needed each other so much. When a break in the conversation gave her a chance, Elizabeth leapt at it.

"Where is Phillip?" Rythen looked at her, then started to turn away. "I asked you a question and I demand an answer. Where is my mate?"

"He's working on a project. He will be home soon." She stood up and moved toward him. "I don't know what is going on in your head right now, but harming me will not bring him home."
~~~

She stopped. No, it would not, but maybe she could. Raising her arms above her head, she reached out into the world. Everything and anything that could give her just a little of themselves came into her. Electricity cracked between her fingers, and her arms felt the weight of the magic that was hers. Thanking everyone who had given of themselves, she thought of her one true love. "Phillip."

"Christ." Looking around the room, she saw Aaron first. He was rushing around with a blanket in his hands. Then she saw him, her one and only love. And he was as naked as the day he'd been made.

"Hello there, my love. Figured it out, did you?" Phillip took the blanket from Aaron and wrapped it around his waist as he walked toward her. It was apparent that he'd been in the shower. Soap still clung to his hair. His face was filled with humor and love, and she wanted nothing more than to pull him to her and kiss him. But there was the matter of Rythen.

"You shouldn't have been able to do that." She quirked a brow at him. "Nothing in this world is strong enough to support you that way. I'm the only one, and you didn't touch me."

"You think I got this from one being? Or do you think that I stole it? You do, don't you?" His face said that he had. "Well, for your information, I asked and got what I needed. As you made me of both worlds, I govern them both. And as much as you think I've failed, they love me and were more than willing to help me." Elizabeth took Phillip's hand. "I've been thinking about what you're planning for me. And while there is little to nothing I can do to prevent you from doing what you think best, I want you to know that I plan to live my final days with my family. And if you don't like that, you can just fuck the hell off."

When she turned back to Phillip, he was dressed, and they sat down on the couch together. Elizabeth had never felt so good in her entire life. When Duncan came in with his tray, she smiled up at him when he handed her a large glass of sweet tea.

"My lady. Sire. I see that things are the way they should be once again. Will you be staying for dinner? I do believe we are having roasted chicken with all the bulbs." It took her several seconds to figure out what he meant.

"Trimmings. And yes, that would be lovely." He winked at her and offered Phillip a glass as well. When he turned to Aaron, Duncan smiled before speaking. "Sire, there is all manner of people in the kitchen. Master Colin is very…I would say he is displeased, but that would be an understatement. Lady Sara is working to calm him, but there are the others. Lady Shade has also threatened to cut some…parts off the young man who is flirting with her, and then there is Lady Maddie. I do believe she has gotten better with her magic in recent days."

"Others, Duncan? It sounds as if you have a few visitors there. That kitchen is pretty big. Just how many others are there?" Duncan flushed at his master, and Elizabeth put her hand over her mouth to stifle the laugh she felt bubbling up. "Duncan, you're scaring me."

"All that could fit, sire. And then some. The faeries have taken to the ceiling so as not to be smashed. The brownies and the pixies are…. Sire, I do believe there is a war going to come from this." He looked to the kitchen when a crash sounded. "I believe that was my new mixer. Someone will need to replace that posthaste."

As Duncan moved toward the kitchen, Aaron did as well. Logan didn't move but sat in the chair looking for all the world like he had not a trouble in the world. Rythen was staring at him, and it took Elizabeth a few seconds to realize that they were speaking.

"It is considered rude to talk in a foreign language when there are others about. I'm sure the same could be said for telepathy conversations." Logan looked at her and smiled. "And you, sir, look as if you might have solved some great mystery."

"I do believe I have." Logan stood up and took her hand. After kissing it, he looked to Phillip. "Have you finished the book? Mathew will be thrilled to death that you're home by the way. And he has a great deal more pictures to add to his book the two of you are creating for future generations."

"I have only just. And pictures? I'm so happy to hear that he has not quit his job. I've a great need to see him as well. Did you know that some of the things that I've been working on were a good deal easier because of that scamp? Oh my, I would so love to see him again, and the other children. And I am to understand that congratulations are in order…a new baby to hold. How wonderful for us all." Logan nodded and turned to Rythen.

"You are only welcome here because I have stood up for you. Fuck this up and I'll make sure that you are in a world of hurt. There will be no more talk of this ending shit either. You have a question, a statement concerning it, you come to me. Understand?" Logan looked like a man who was thrice his size. Magic, as powerful magic as he held, would do that. Rythen wanted to be impressed, but he was more angry than anything.

"You should have more respect for me." Logan snorted at Rythen. "I'm a good deal older than you and a tad more on the strong side. I could end your very existence with a snap of my finger."

"First of all, respect is earned, and you, sir, have not earned a thing from me. Secondly, if you really thought you could end me, as you put it, I do believe you would have by now. We both know that you cannot." Logan put his hands on his hips as he continued. "I've read the entire contract. You should know that I am well aware of things now. And the few loopholes that you put in for yourself will benefit me when I need them. You, sir, are royally fucked."

Rythen looked at her before looking back at Logan. There was something there. Something both of them knew but were not sharing. But before she could ask or even look, the room was suddenly filled with people. Colin picked her up in a large hug and kissed her soundly on the cheek. Elizabeth squealed with delight. She so loved the big man.

"My lady. I'd heard that ye'd been harmed. And then when I felt your request for help, I knew that there were lies abounding." He looked over at Rythen, who stood up. "Ye'd be better off standing down. I've no use for a mon such as you. To think I thought you a good person."

"It's not right that I'm being judged for something that was created long ago. This contract is something that we both agreed upon." Rythen turned to her. "I will not be the subject of all this. You and I know that this will end for you. I'm not the only one at fault. You signed the contract as well."

"I did. When there was no family for me. No mate to love, children to hold onto. And you said that I would rule for a time and when that time was up, I'd be able to live out my days in a ring with the faeries to watch over me. You never once said a thing about having children. You lied to me."

Her temper was getting up, and several of the people in the room took a step back. It wasn't until Lizzy stood in front of her that she started to calm. There was something so serene about her that....

"You're with child." Lizzy nodded and smiled. "Oh my child, you've made me so happy. Does your father know?"

"No. Would you like to tell him? Logan is afraid of him. You know, daddy seems to think we're not having sex." Elizabeth hugged her granddaughter to her and told her she'd be thrilled to tell the old poo. "Just wait until the moment is right, okay?"

"You mean when Logan is nowhere near him?" Lizzy laughed and told her yes. "I will enjoy this. More than you can imagine."

As soon as Aaron sat down with his friends and family around him, she knew this was it. At some point Rythen had left, and she was glad. News like this was for family, and he most certainly wasn't.

"I'd like to make an announcement." She looked at Aaron. "You're so going to love me for this. Lizzy is going to make you a grandda again."

The look on his face was something she would remember for the rest of her life. He looked thrilled beyond words for about ten seconds. Then his face changed to one of complete fury. When he stood up, Logan did as well. The two of them were going to have to work this out, but for now, she was going to enjoy the show.

"I told you that we were having monkey sex whenever we could." Aaron growled at Logan, who laughed. "How on earth do you think Mac had a child? I'm pretty sure that they were having sex all the time—"

"He's not my daughter." Logan laughed harder and backed up as Aaron continued. "You told me that I could trust you. You said you'd take care of her."

"I'm pretty sure I did. A lot. She really enjoyed herself a great deal. If you asked her, I'm sure she'd tell you the same thing. We really like sex." Logan was still laughing when Aaron grabbed him around the throat. It wasn't until Lizzy put her hand on her dad's arm that he let him go.

"I'm not happy with him." Lizzy told her dad that she knew, but that she loved him. "That is the only reason that I've not murdered him."

"But you're going to be a grandda again. And also, I wanted to tell you that the adoption went through. We're going to get the four boys that I was telling you about. We will get them this afternoon."

As Aaron hugged Lizzy and shook Logan's hand, all Elizabeth could think about was that there would be more children. Elizabeth felt her heart break a little, and she looked at Phillip. "We're going to have to love them as much as we can."

"We will anyway. Now, no more thoughts about this thing with Rythen. We have a big family coming and we're going to enjoy it as much as they'll let us." He stood up. "I think we need to go shopping. I believe a large party is set for tonight, and we'll bring them gifts."

The two of them left with all the family congratulating the young couple. Mathew showed up just as they were leaving and they asked if he could go with them. Of course they said he could, and the little man was so happy he hugged them several times on the way out to the car.

"What do you think of having new brothers?" Phillip smiled at Mathew when he only shrugged. "You don't want brothers? Or do you want sisters instead?"

"Oh I guess they'll be okay. They're vampires, did you know that? And one of them is older than me. Not a lot, but a few weeks." He looked out the window as he continued. "I guess Grandda will want to spend a lot of time with him because they're the same and all."

"I doubt that. He might love the new children a great deal, but you forget that you were the first one to call him that. I'm pretty sure that you and Aaron will have a very special relationship forever." Phillip smiled. "You don't think we're going to spend more time with them, do you?"

"I don't know. They're going to live forever and I'm not." Elizabeth looked at Phillip, and he smiled. They needed to tell him.

"You're going to live for a very long time as well. We've…your grandmother and I have been putting a little extra in your body for months now. We did it a little at a time so no one would get upset with us. But you should live another…oh I don't know, a few thousand years, so long as you don't do anything stupid." Mathew shook his head. "You don't believe me?"

"Yes, I believe you. And I know all about it. And Mom and Dad know too. They told me you'd been supercharging me." Mathew climbed over the seat of the limo and hugged Phillip. "I'm glad you are. I would really miss you if I had to go so soon. And Dad said that it made me special because nobody else was going to be as powerful as me. But he said I had to be careful that my juices wouldn't kick in until I was older."

Elizabeth knew that was true. What Mathew had now was enough to do some serious magic if he were to use it, but he was still human. Elizabeth hugged him to her and gave him another gift, one that would protect him for the rest of his human life. And maybe poor Duncan would be a little more relaxed as well. Phillip touched her mind as she watched the two of them together.

"I'm glad you did that. It makes me feel better just knowing that he'll be safe. We should start his training then. It would be nice for him to use this if the need came. I think he will do well with the right training. What do you think?"

Instead of answering him, she looked at Mathew. "Starting tomorrow morning, I'd like for you to come to the castle, and Grandda and I will begin your magic training. I'm pretty sure I still have the books that your mother used. It might be fun for the three of us. And I'm pretty sure that Mel's children can help you as well. Why, just the other day I saw little Grace making a messenger mist. You'll need one of those as well."

The rest of the trip to the mall was made with much speculation on what he would do first. Mathew was such a treasure to them, as were all the children. But this little boy would hold a special place in their hearts because of his father. Logan had done so much for them.

CHAPTER 6

Rythen sat on his bed and thought about all that was going on. And if he was truthful to himself he was a little afraid. When he'd returned to the castle, the woman was gone, yet her scent was everywhere. She had been back in his room and if he wasn't mistaken, she'd managed to touch everything in there. He picked up the pillow that lay over his lap and brought it to his nose. Her scent was strongest there.

A mate. He knew now that she was just that. A human mate was not something that he had planned for. And worse yet, she was mad at him. He glanced at the note that had been on his desk when he'd returned from the other realm and thought about what she'd said.

"Stay away from me. And if you think I'm kidding, you just try and come near me again. I've no more use for you than you do me. Double that. I think you're insane as well."

There had been nothing else other than her name. Kim Craft. At least now he knew the name of the woman who would haunt him for the rest of his life. Moving to the window, he watched the faeries move along the darkened field. He had seen it when he'd first come to the castle and wondered about it. One of the pixies told him what had happened.

"Megan the Black did it. She had been told over and over not to go there to do her practicing. And over the months of her not listening to anyone, she destroyed it all. The queen tried to repair it, but there was no help for it. She said that it was dead very deep and that it would be centuries before she could try again." The little pixie moved to just the edge of the forest. "My mom worked there, as did my dad. They said it was beautiful once."

"What happened to this Megan the Black? Was she punished?" She smiled and nodded. "Good. There should have been a trial as well for her actions."

There had been, she'd told him. Not only had Megan destroyed a large field, but she had kidnapped one of the Royal court. And for that she'd been hanged. Rythen was impressed that her punishment had been just and that it had been carried out so swiftly.

Rythen walked out of the castle a few minutes later and found Draco sunning in the yard. The smaller creatures seemed to be all over him, and when Rythen asked him why, he laughed.

"They find my warmth to be at odds with what I am. I would guess that I'd be cold, but the sun here keeps my scales warm, and they love it." He opened one eye and looked at him without raising his head. "You seem to be in a low kind of spirit. Perhaps you should find a sunny spot and rest it away."

"I was thinking I need your help with something." Rythen pointed to the dark forest. "I can repair that but will need you to help me. I was thinking that it would be nice for the other faeries to go if they wanted. You as well."

"I would be honored to bring back what was lost to us. Lady Elizabeth cried for months over the destruction.

She felt the loss of the faeries that had been caught in the fire as if it were her own children. There was a memorial put up in their honor that she visits daily." Something else the pixie had told him. What an honorable and kind woman Elizabeth was.

They moved slowly to the field. Not because of the distance, for it was only a few short miles away, but because Draco didn't want to disturb the forest he was in. There were as many above the ground, he'd told him, as below. He had to tread softly.

"They tend to get a little upset with me when I accidently crush a tree or two. And if there is a flower that had been set for propagation, then I never hear the end of it. No, it is better for all if I walk as if I walk on eggs."

The damage was extensive. And as they walked through the brittle ground, he wondered if he'd be able to fix it after all. When Draco said his name, Rythen looked at him.

"'Tis a great sadness here. I don't think I've ever felt something so profound before. Can you work some magic on it?" Rythen wasn't sure, but he wanted to try. "I've summoned you some help. I hope you don't mind."

Rythen looked up to see not just Melody coming toward him, but the rest of the family as well. Even a few of the vampires were there, as well as Tess and her mate. They looked ready to do business.

"Where do we start?" Melody looked out over the field. "I can summon a great deal of magic from the surrounding areas, and Mom and Grandmother a bit more. These men and women have said to take from them as well."

Logan appeared with Aaron and Sara, and as he watched, she organized a long chain of magic with the others by having them hold hands. The power was enough to supply a very large state, but he wasn't sure it was enough to completely heal the earth beyond them. When Duncan appeared a few minutes later getting the faeries to bring drinks and food, Rythen felt something he'd not felt in all his considerable years. He felt the power of love and friendship.

"We'll do this. It will drain us badly, I think, but I do believe it can be done." He was startled to see young Mathew snapping pictures of the devastation. He wanted to see some of his work, but knew that he had to concentrate on the task at hand. Rythen looked at Elizabeth when she stepped near him. "He will record this for history?"

"Yes, and he will do a fine job of it as well." Elizabeth put out her hand as she spoke to him. "We're ready when you are."

Reaching for her hand, he nearly let her go as soon as they touched. It was as if he'd touched something electrified. When she nodded to him, Rythen looked out over the field and pulled the power being fed to him, and little by little he felt it come into him. Then Elizabeth touched his mind.

"I'm giving you it in small doses. Too much will hurt you, and this way you won't drain us too quickly. Let her rip when you're ready." Rythen nodded and pushed the magic outward.

At first he felt nothing, just the power running though him like he was a conduit. He knew the exact moment when someone else touched his source and it soared through him and outward like a hose. Closing his eyes, Rythen willed the forest to take what was freely offered and to use it.

He had no idea how long he had used this magic. Rythen did know that he was nearing his end when Elizabeth let go of him. Unable to stand, he crumpled to the ground and lay there. Had anyone tried to harm him at that moment, he would have had to let them. He was as drained as he'd ever been. The glass of juice that was shoved into his hands was just what he needed, but he didn't have the strength to lift it to his mouth. He heard someone say his name and looked up at them. Aaron.

"You'll have to drink this before Duncan has a fit. He said that you were to have three glasses of this vile stuff before I was to put you to bed." The first sip of the nectar was heavenly cool. "That's it, drink it down."

"Did it work?" Aaron laughed and told him he could see something but not a great deal right now. "It will take centuries to regrow."

Aaron laughed again, but Rythen was too weak to care. As soon as he closed his eyes, he felt his body go lax. Exhaustion seemed to not just move over him, but had taken up residence as well. Sleep claimed him immediately.

~~~

Kim tried her best to hide the bruises on her face. Josh had been so mad at her last night that she was sure he was going to kill her. She should have called and told him she was going to be late.

The truth of the matter was she'd not given him a single thought once she'd sat with those women. They had talked to her for hours, and the time had just sped by. They had told her all sorts of things that she knew couldn't be true, but they believed it, so she simply smiled at them. But the woman who had given her the lift home had told her the most amazing news. Elizabeth had told
~~~

her that all of them had enjoyed her and wanted to get together soon. Kim had never had any female friends before, and since Josh, not even many male ones. She had missed them.

When the elevator opened, she put her hand over her cheek to try to hide the cut. But Ms. Lizzy pulled her hand away and glared at it.

"He was most upset with me because I didn't call and tell him I was going to be late." Lizzy snorted. "I should have thought about how much he'd miss me. I'm not saying it's my fault entirely, but I was late and I didn't call."

"Missed you as a punching bag, you mean. You know that slimy bastard needs to pick a fight with me. I'll show him what it's like to be hit." Kim wanted to be upset with her, but she was more embarrassed than anything. When she sat down in the chair across from her, Kim put her hands under the desk. If she saw the bruises on her arms, she might fire her.

"I'm not going to fire you." Kim nodded, relieved. "There are a great many things I'd like to do for you right now, but this will have to do."

The touch was gentle and warm. As soon as Lizzy's fingers moved down her cheek and over her arms, she felt as if she'd been given something strong to take away the pain. When she put her hand to her cheek, Kim was startled to find that the wound there was gone, as was the pain. She looked at Lizzy and all she did was shrug.

"I need a favor from you." Kim nodded and said anything. "I would refrain from being so generous if I were you, but I do need some help with something. I know you had fun at the castle last night. Grandma said you might still not believe everything, but she thought you were coming around."

Kim grinned. "Draco gave me a ride on his back. I've never even been in a plane, and he took me so high. I'm not sure about the rest, but I'm not going to be as closed-minded as I once was."

"Good for you. And I'm assuming you didn't tell the prick who hit you either?" Kim shook her head. "I didn't think you would. And you should know that if you did tell him, he'd more than likely take something of your happiness away. Don't let him hurt you again."

Kim had a feeling she wasn't just talking about the physical hurts either, but the way he cut her down all the time. And then there was the money. She blurted out what he'd told her before he'd hit her the last few times.

"He took all my money. I went to the bank this morning to get a money order for our rent and it's all gone. I hadn't even signed off on the paper saying he could get into it yet and they gave it to him." Lizzy picked up her phone and pressed some buttons. "You're not having him arrested, are you?"

"No, nothing that simple. But a friend of mine can take care of the money being returned." Lizzy started talking to a woman by the name of Miss Pete. "I'd like for you to see what you can find out about an account for me. Kim Craft had her money in one of our banks, and they let an unauthorized person take out the money."

Ten minutes later, Lizzy hung up. "She said to tell you that no one will get into your account again, and that the bank is going to pay your rent this month as well. It's the least they can do. Also, you should know that as of now, your account is quite a bit more than you started with. As I said before, I need your help."

"Anything." Even though she'd been cautioned about it, she would sincerely do anything for this woman. This woman had saved her from being tossed out on her ass. The landlord had told her that if she was late again, he would have no choice but to kick her out. He was already mad that Josh was living there with her and his name wasn't on the lease.

"You might not think so when you hear what it is. You remember Rythen?" She nodded and felt her face heat up. The man could touch her in ways no man ever had before. "I need someone to watch over him for me. He's...he's ill."

"Oh my. Did something happen to him? It wasn't Draco, was it? I know the dragon would never really harm anyone, and Mr. Rythen might just be out of sorts about something."

"He's saved a forest." Kim didn't understand how that would happen, but since meeting these people, she'd been subject to a lot of things she didn't understand. Nodding, she told her she'd watch him until he was better. Before she could ask her when she would start, Kim found herself back at the castle.

"He's very weak, so I don't expect him to wake for several days." Kim barely heard Lizzy talk...she was too busy looking at the man on the bed. "He drained himself pretty good helping out the forest, so he might be down for a while."

"He's very pale, isn't he?" Kim wanted to move his hair from his brow but was afraid of waking him. He seemed to be in such a deep sleep that he didn't appear to be breathing. "How will he receive fluids? He will need them, won't he?"

"He will, but I doubt that he'll wake enough to take them in. What I need for you to do is just to make sure that if he does wake, there is someone here to give him what he needs." Kim looked around the large room she'd been in before when Lizzy told her that everything she needed was there. "Just go to the door there and anyone of the guards watching over this room will see that you have whatever you need. And don't worry that they won't have it. We can produce anything you want."

"I'll be here at nights then." Lizzy nodded, and Kim wondered what would happen to her when she returned to Josh. "He'll not be happy."

"You let me worry about Josh. I've got it on good authority that he won't even miss you from where he'll be." Kim started to ask what that meant but was sure she didn't want to know. Lizzy would take care of him and that would be it. The woman was amazing.

After Lizzy left her, Kim sat down on the big chair next to the bed. Rythen didn't move when she sat up and finally moved the hair from his brow. He was simply too handsome with that rakish hair out of place.

"You're much too handsome as it is, and I think you know it." She looked around the room to make sure she was alone. When she was sure she was, Kim continued to talk to the sleeping man.

"You kiss like it's your job. While I haven't been kissed a great deal, I've been kissed by some pretty amazing men. They never made me feel like you did." She flushed when her body heated up again. "You should be ashamed of yourself treating me that way. And we not even knowing each other."

The knock at the door startled her, and she went to open it. The man standing there had her staring at him stupidly. He only smiled and asked to enter.

"I'm just what you think me to be, a centaur. My name is Roman. I was born here long ago when our kind was in a large number, but humans no longer believed in us so we became nearly extinct. I stayed on after my family was moved to another glen to help bring us back around." He sat a large tray on the table near the window. "If you are not happy with our selections, then please let me know. I've been working on some of the finer recipes that I have gotten from Master Duncan."

Kim sat down when he pulled out her chair and smiled at him. She had met Duncan right after being hired to work for Logan. He didn't strike her as a culinary type. But then she was sort of hungry. The first cover was lifted, and she looked at the food, then at the man.

"You are not happy with this?" He started to take the tray back, and she put her hand on his. The electrical current that ran between them had her jerking back.

"It's wonderful. I love…this is one of my bucket list meals." He looked at her oddly. "I never get to go out, and when I cook at the apartment, Josh gets…well, he gets sort of out of joint about it. So I came up with a list of foods that I want to try before I die. I think this was on the top."

Lobster bisque with rice and asparagus was on the first plate. When Roman unwrapped the basket, she could smell the crust-covered bread that smelled so yeasty that her mouth watered. Under the last cover was a slice of the thickest cherry pie she'd ever seen. And there was a bowl of the cream he'd told her to go with it.

"The cherries were picked just today for the queen's dessert. She said that you should have a slice as well. My

Lady Queen is the most generous of people." He poured her a glass of what looked like blood, but he assured her it was only wine. After he left, she bit into the most scrumptious meal she'd ever eaten. If she ate like this for her lunch, she wondered what they would serve for dinner.

"If this keeps up I'll weigh a ton when I get back home." Finishing off the meal, she laid back on the chair, too full to move. Kim yawned twice before she got up to check on her patient. He was still sleeping soundly.

"I'm not sure what I'm supposed to do with you." Several thoughts popped into her head and none of them had anything to do with his well-being, and more to do with him being naked. "I wonder where that thought came from, and if you're somehow making me feel this way." She felt stupid after saying it and snapped her mouth closed. No more talking to the sleeping man, she decided.

After Roman came to get her empty plates, she started to wander around the room. She was on her second pass when she sat down again. She was so tired that she could hardly keep her eyes open. In moments, she was asleep, and the dream started almost immediately.

"You're not supposed to be here." Rythen looked like a god lying across his bed. Instead of being dressed in the shirt she'd seen him in, he was naked from the waist up. It took her mind several seconds to realize that he was laughing at her.

"You shouldn't be invading my dreams. I'm too tired to mess with you right now." He nodded and started to sit up. "Oh, no you don't. If you're as naked as I think you are, you just stay right there."

"But I want you." She shook her head and started to move. How she'd gotten so close to the bed was beyond her, but he was pulling her toward him. "If you won't let me come to you, I will bring you to me."

His mouth was covering hers even as he rolled her to her back. Heat filled her body as he touched her throat and breast. When he cupped her ass and brought her close to him, she moaned out his name. His cock was so hard she could feel it through the blankets he was under.

"Let me taste you. It will go a long way toward healing me for you." She didn't think she'd live if he was healed any more and nearly told him so. "I could wake and do this and so much more to you if you would allow it." He nipped at her throat, and she curled her fingers into his hair.

"You're making me crazy with need." He chuckled against her throat, and she moaned again. "What do you need from me? I mean, how do you taste me?"

Her mind went in all sorts of directions when she thought of him tasting her. The one and only time she'd finally gotten Josh to go down on her, he'd hurt her so badly that she'd cried for an hour. But she doubted very much that anything that Rythen did to her would hurt at all.

"I would never harm you." His mouth moved down her throat to her breast. It wasn't until his warm breath was touching her flesh that she realized he'd removed her blouse and bra. Then his tongue moved over her nipple.

"Please, I need you to help me to come. I just need a little relief." He lifted his head from her breast, and she whimpered. "You're going to leave me like this, aren't you? Josh does that. He thinks—"

Rythen put his fingers over her mouth. "Never speak of another man again when you're with me. I will give you pleasure, but you've not answered me. May I taste of you?"

"You can have all of me if you won't leave me hanging." He looked deep into her eyes, and she felt as if he were looking into her soul. "You won't hurt me either, will you?"

"Never." Lowering his head to her throat again, Kim felt his tongue run along her pulse. She was almost embarrassed by how hard it must be pounding, and started to move her head so that he'd not feel it. But he nipped at her, and her body reacted like he'd touched her with a live wire. Her climax tore from her so quickly and hard that she could have sworn that she saw stars. And when he suckled at her, Kim wanted more.

"You'll give me all as you promised, my love." His voice in her head didn't even bother her. When he lifted his head, she could see her blood on his lip and wanted to taste him the same way. "Think of biting me. You'll need fangs to do that, and I'd very much like to feel you drink from me as well."

Her mouth burst in pain, but it was short lived. When Rythen moved over her body, she felt his cock just at her entrance and rolled her hips to take him in. He slammed forward so hard that he took her breath away. And when he stilled deep inside of her, she looked up at him.

"This is no dream, is it?" He rolled his hips as she'd done and she had to grab onto him before she came apart again. "I want to come, and the need to bite you is making me hungry for it."

"Then by all means, you should do it." He moved again, and she was so close to coming that she was panting with need. "When you come, love, I want you to bite me deep. Sink your teeth into me and drink. I will keep you safe."

The thought of biting him had her dizzy with the need to do so. When he moved inside of her, his body slamming deep, so much so that she knew she'd be sore if this were real, she felt her orgasm swallow her. It took her over and when she felt his neck just there for her, she ran her tongue down to his pounding pulse and sank her teeth into him.

Blood filled her mouth, and when she drank him down, her body hummed with sudden energy. The connection to him was amazing. Her climax hurled her into another one as she suckled at his neck. And when he pulled her wrist to his mouth and bit her, Kim knew that whatever sort of dream this was, she hoped that she would have it nightly. Nothing had ever made her feel this way, and she knew that had she really been in bed with him, no one would ever make her feel this way again. Kim was his.

CHAPTER 7

Elizabeth moved down the hall to speak to Rythen. There were only a few days left, and she needed to see if he'd give her an extension to see Lizzy's baby born. If he did that she'd not give him any more troubles but go willingly to her death. She was rounding the corner to his chamber when she felt the floor beneath her tremble.

She met Mel coming from the council room and could see that she had no idea what had happened either. They both moved toward Rythen's room, where shouting could be heard. They were nearly there when something came crashing out of the room. It took them several seconds to realize it was a vase. The amount of shattered pieces made her realize it was a very large piece at that.

"You will not leave this room until we have spoken about your need to ignore what had happened between us." Rythen was angry about something, and Elizabeth was glad for once it wasn't aimed at her. But the next voice had her running to the room only to be brought up short by the woman coming out.

"I am not going to sleep with you. That was a fucking dream." Kim sounded very unsure of herself and looked up at her when she was steady on her feet. "Please tell me that I didn't just drink blood from him during the most incredible sex of my life. Please?"

Mel went in first, and Elizabeth led Kim back in. The room was a shambles, and Rythen looked like he might have caught a few of the pieces, that now lay around the room, with his head. Elizabeth had to fight hard not to laugh at him.

"She is my mate. And I suppose that none of you had anything to do with this?" Mel asked him what. "With her being here, in my bed?"

"I was not in your bed, you fucking idiot. As I have said to you several times, I never had sex with you. It was a dream." Elizabeth nearly burst out laughing when Rythen reached for Kim, only to have her slap him away. "I told you not to touch me. I want to go home. Now."

"Lizzy brought her here." Elizabeth looked at Mel as she explained. "She thought that it would be good for her to get away from her boyfriend for a few days. And because you were so out of it, we both thought it would be a good way to get her here by asking her to watch over you. What the hell are you doing awake? You should have been down for at least a week."

"She fed me." Everyone looked at Kim and she paled a good deal more than she already was. "Get her something to eat before she passes out. I might have taken a little too much from her."

Mel only quirked a brow at him. He told her he was sorry, but she was pale. Shamus came into the room with a servant who was pushing a large cart filled with juices and fruit.

"Here you go, my dear. And not because he has commanded you to do so, I think it would be best if you ate a bit, and drank down as much of the juice as you can." Shamus handed her a bottle, and Elizabeth knew that the girl would have no choice but to drink it. Shamus was very good at compelling people to do what he needed without making them feel badly about it. Kim was drinking her second glass when Aaron came into the room.

"I came as soon as I got your message." He looked at Rythen, then at Shamus. "Did he rape her? I'll kill him if he did."

"No." Kim stood up and moved between Aaron and Rythen. "He didn't rape me because nothing happened. I had a very erotic dream and now I'd very much like to go home. Josh will be—"

The growl coming from Rythen surprised her. Elizabeth looked at Kim. If she didn't know better, she would think that they really had mated. Reaching out to touch the girl's head, she had her answer. They were truly one.

Even before she spoke, Kim was shaking her head. "I swear to you it was just a dream. Very detailed and very wonderful, but only a dream. I didn't grow fangs, and I didn't drink his blood. Right?"

"I'm sorry, love, but you're his mate." Kim sat down and stared at the floor, and Elizabeth's heart went out to her. The poor thing was in shock. When Rythen moved to stand beside her, Aaron took him by the shoulder and turned him around.

"Did you tell her what you were doing before you mated with her?" Rythen tried to brush him off, but Aaron was a good deal stronger than he looked. "I asked you a question. Did you tell her?"

"No. And so what if I didn't? She's my mate, and thanks to your meddling daughter she is now a part of me. I wanted—" Rythen sailed across the room and hit the far wall with such force the plaster held him in place as Aaron made his way to him again. He only stopped when Shamus stepped in front of him.

"I'm going to kill him." Shamus shook his head at Aaron and moved him back. "The man raped her. He not only raped her body, but he took what was not freely given. He needs to be punished."

"And he will. But not in front of the girl." Everyone turned to Kim when Shamus spoke in low tones. "Take her to your home and protect her. I'm sure there are any number of things you can do to keep her safe. Do not let her return home until you hear from me. This only may be a matter of seeing what really happened here."

"I don't like this." Neither man looked at Rythen as he slid to the floor. He still hadn't woken up this time, and Aaron turned to Kim. "Come, child. I'll make sure that you're safe, and that we—"

"Take me home. I don't know how you can do it, but I want to go home. Now. I'm sick of this crap and the way you guys keep shuffling me all over the place. It's time…I want to go home." Elizabeth was suddenly afraid for her, but they had no choice. Short of putting her into a deep sleep and keeping her that way until they got to the bottom of this, they could not make her do a thing…especially now that she was mated to Rythen.

Aaron nodded and took her hand. When they both disappeared, Elizabeth watched as Shamus picked up her creator and tossed him unceremoniously onto the bed. If the man wasn't sore after this, it would be a miracle.

"He did mate with her. And whether or not she knew is pointless now." Elizabeth sat down on the chair as Shamus ordered Rythen to be chained down. It would do them little good, but at least it might slow him a bit. "What do you suppose she meant by it being only a dream?"

"He was in a deep, restful sleep when I checked on him before Lizzy brought Kim here. I never thought of him being able to dream walk with her. Had they done anything before this?" Elizabeth told Mel that she thought Kim and Rythen had kissed. "Well, it must have been enough for him to do it then. Why he'd do this to her is beyond me. And she might not be thinking she was willing now, but she must have enjoyed it somewhat."

Elizabeth knew for the bond to work they both would have had to have been climaxing. There could be no faking that either. It had to be from the heart and body. She looked up at Mel when she spoke again.

"What do we do about her now? That boyfriend of hers will kill her if he finds out about this. And Lizzy said that he's not to be arrested until sometime tomorrow. The police should have done this when he took her money out of the bank two days ago." Elizabeth knew that the man was violent, and he would hurt her if given only the slightest of reasons.

"I think we should simply bring her to Aaron's and keep her there. We know he can protect her." Mel was shaking her head even as Elizabeth finished speaking. "He has to follow the rules like we all do."

"I'm afraid so." Rythen stirred, and they both looked over at him. Shamus hadn't moved from the side of the bed, and when Rythen demanded that he be freed, Shamus looked at her.

"Mel has turned you over to me." She hadn't, but when he looked at Mel, she nodded. "From now on you'll listen to me or else. The girl has gone to her home, and until I'm satisfied that you're going to leave her alone, you'll stay there."

"She's my mate, not some harlot that I fucked. I want her brought here now." Elizabeth only sat still as Rythen ranted for several more minutes. Shamus left her alone with him, taking Mel and the guard with him.

"But I'll be close enough to come to your aid should you need me." Shamus looked at Rythen as he continued. "You make me come back here and so help me, you'll wish that you could die."

She waited for him to speak. There was no reason for him to talk to her at all, she knew, but now that it had been established that she was in charge of him, no one could help him even if she thought anyone would.

"Where is she?" Elizabeth had been thinking of the first time she'd seen Phillip when Rythen finally spoke. "Where is Kim now?"

"Home. She demanded that Aaron take her there, and as your mate, he has no choice but to listen to her." Elizabeth got up and moved to the window to look at the new forest. "It's nearly complete. All the faeries have been planting seedlings for hours and some of them are already sprouting."

"I didn't think it would work." She nodded as a large tree started to spread its branches and reach for the sky. "There was a great deal of power given freely today. I wonder why they would help me."

"They didn't. I asked and they said they'd do anything for me." She glanced at him before looking out the window. "I know you have a low opinion of the way I ran things, but everyone here seems to like me. And would, as you've found out, do anything I ask of them."

"I'm beginning to see that." He shifted on the bed, and she put a pillow behind his head. "Thank you."

"Kim is living with an abusive boyfriend. He hits her a great deal, and one day I fear he'll kill her. She will not leave him because she feels that she deserves no more than him." Elizabeth thought of her own mate and knew that he'd die before he caused her any hurt. "Her father abused her, as well as anyone that thought to make themselves feel better by hitting her. She's very…I was going to say fragile, but I don't think that word suits when she is with you."

"No, she has no problem standing up to me." Elizabeth continued to watch the field. It was coming along so nicely, and the flowers that had been planted just that afternoon were sprouting true leaves. The trees, which were saplings that had been taken from Avalon, were doing well too. She turned to Rythen.

"I remember meeting Phillip the first time as if it were yesterday. He'd been watching over a man you'd brought in to see to something." Rythen nodded, smiling. "Do you remember him?"

"Yes. He was a pompous fool. He actually told me that making the seer of magic a woman would be a grave mistake. I told him someone needed to be there who would have a temper to match mine and would have a will to only rule. I guess I did well in that area with you." He looked at the painting in the wall of the Tree of Life. "I never meant for you to have children."

She sat down. Never have…? "Why not? And if you didn't, then how did I have Mathew and Savannah?"

"Those damned Fates. I had told them what I was doing, that coming up with a woman to rule forever would be the only way to make the worlds work. We knew that there would be problems. But a continuity throughout the centuries would have made dealing with them so much better." He looked at her. "I was gone but ten minutes. And when I returned, I knew they had done something but had never…it wasn't until I returned after Mathew was born that I realized what had happened. Then when Savannah was born some years later, I knew it was for the best. They made you happy."

"They made me very happy. And how do you feel about Mel? Do you think she could run the kingdom without guidance?" She waited for him to answer, but when he didn't, she stood up. "You can admit that you've made a mistake. It will change nothing. You're still going to end my life."

"It was a mistake."

Those four words meant more to her than she thought possible. Elizabeth knew that he'd not change his mind about the other. And when he didn't continue, she stood to watch the progress again. In the few minutes that she'd looked away, so much had changed.

"When I created Avalon to have a place to go, I never dreamed it would come to mean so much to so many. Tess and her mate have lived there these past decades, and their children have come to mean so much to me. Draco can be found flying over the castle, and the unicorns are there as well. They have repopulated and we have a whole new generation of them." Elizabeth grinned at the antics of the brownies as they chased after the wolves that were running through their work. "Most of the children that are of Aaron's kiss have been there as well. Some have even decided to stay on to help with the magic there."

"It will still be there." Elizabeth nodded and felt a small nudge of something. It took her moments to realize it was Kim, the girl.

"She's in trouble." Looking at Rythen, she could see that he knew as well. "If I release you to go to her, what will you do?"

"Kill him." Elizabeth looked out the window. "You'll not release me to go to her? She is my mate."

Elizabeth finished her conversation with Aaron before answering. "I've sent Aaron. He'll make sure that she is all right. And he'll take her back to his home to ensure that she has nothing else happen to her."

"I need to see her. Not that I think Aaron won't do as you wish, but I need to see her." Elizabeth moved toward the door as Rythen yelled for her to stop. "You're doing this as revenge, aren't you? I have news for you, whether or not you let me go, you are still going to leave this life. I cannot change that."

"I'm well aware of what you plan to do. But releasing you now would harm the balance between Molavonta and the humans. She will be safer, as will the others that would be close to her, if you are not released on them. Not yet at any rate. You will need to calm a good deal more before we can have you loose." She moved out of the door and into the hallway with him still screaming at her. It had to be the hardest thing she'd ever done.

By the time she made it to the hospital, Kim was already in surgery. Elizabeth thought about going back to get Rythen, but decided that he'd still use his considerable magic, and it just couldn't be done. Not with all the humans around. Aaron took her to the front desk.

"They need someone to be responsible for her." Elizabeth nodded. "I know that you and she are close, but right now I'm not able to do this without harming a few people."

His beast had risen, and Elizabeth put her hand to his heart to calm him. When he nodded to her, she turned to speak to the nurse. There were papers that needed to be signed and insurance information to be given. The doctor was coming toward her when Elizabeth was finishing that up.

"I'm sorry, but she's had some extensive trauma done to her body. I've treated her before and she never let on that it was the boyfriend. A fall here or a mugging once. But this time he…well, he has hit her with something that I can only surmise to be more than his fists. The damage done to her…." He looked away, and Elizabeth was frightened. "If she makes it through the night, she will have a better chance, but…."

"Logan, I need for you go to the castle and bring Rythen here. Tell him to behave or I will not allow him to help Kim. She is dying." Logan said he'd be there in seconds, and Elizabeth looked at the doctor. "The man who hit her isn't a boyfriend but an ex-lover. She had left him for someone else a while ago, and I guess he didn't take it as well as we'd hoped."

"Where is she?" Elizabeth shook her head at Rythen when he stood just to her right. The doctor looked startled but said nothing. Rythen turned to him. "Where is she, and when can I see her?"

The doctor walked away when Elizabeth told him to with her mind. There was no point in everyone hearing what she had to say. When Rythen started to follow, she took his arm. "You'll calm down or so help me I'll have Aaron change her, and he'll own your ass too. She will need you to be calm as well. Take some deep breaths and

I'll take you to her. As of right now, they're not giving her until morning to live. Do you want to have her as your mate forever, or do you wish now that I have one of the others—?"

"Anyone else touches her and I will kill them." Elizabeth nodded. "Please take me to her. I can feel her pain, and her heart is slowing."

The trek down the hall was made quietly. She had pulled the shadows around them much the way vampires do when they don't want anyone to see them. When they entered the recovery room, Elizabeth looked at Kim in shock.

"He's hurt her so badly." Her head was bandaged from crown to chin. All that showed of her face was her mouth, and that had a tube running out of it, and a bright red stain filled it. Her left arm was in a cast, and the right had steel rods running through it to no doubt hold it together.

Her legs were draped in bloodied wraps, and Elizabeth could see that one of them was nearly crushed. A sheet covered her torso, but even that looked like it was stained with blood. Elizabeth wondered aloud how the girl had lived this long.

"It's because of my blood. I exchanged it with her when we mated. I wish now that I had given her more." Elizabeth moved to the bed and looked down at the broken woman. "What can I do? My mind is locked down with seeing her like this."

"Cut your wrist and we'll feed her. I'm not sure how much she'll need, but...let me call Aaron in. He'll know." In seconds her friend was there with them. Aaron had seen her before this, and Elizabeth felt sorry for him. The man, for all his temper, had a heart of gold.

"You'll be able to get her to take a few drops. Once that works through her system, we'll give her more. And you should not be the only one that feeds her." The low growl that came from Rythen had Elizabeth backing up. "I'm sorry. Your blood will heal the wounds, but she needs more than that. She needs for Elizabeth to give her magic as well."

"I have magic." Elizabeth wanted to point out that he had it as well, but Rythen beat her to it. "What does her blood have that mine does not?"

"You are her creator, correct? Well, I'm betting since you've done your part, Elizabeth has taken on a great deal more. Her blood, while yours to begin with is strong, she's made it stronger." Aaron looked at her, then back at Rythen. "You have to give her all that you can for her to live. Is this going to be enough for you not to try? Just because you think you're all that kind of shit?"

Rythen bit into his wrist and put it to Kim's mouth. He glared at Aaron, then looked at her. "I don't know whether or not it will make a difference, but I don't want to take the chance that it doesn't. If you'd be so kind as to help me save my mate, I'd be very grateful to you."

Elizabeth wanted to laugh. It was very hard for her not to, but she nodded and moved to give Kim her blood when Aaron helped her slit open her wrist. She didn't have fangs as they did, but the blade in Aaron's pocket did the trick. As soon as her blood dripped into Kim's mouth, the girl opened her eyes.

"Mom?"

CHAPTER 8

Bradley knew that sooner rather than later the man by the name of Josh Gibson would leave the police station. He was going to enjoy doing this favor for Elizabeth more than he thought necessary. The man would shit himself before this was over, and then Rythen would get his chance. But Aaron was going to get his in first. As soon as David, who'd been put as lookout, came out, Bradley knew the next man would be Gibson.

"You know what really pisses me off? It's the fact that he is blaming her for this. He actually told the police that she had begged him to hit her like this. That she got off on it." David moved toward him as he continued. *"If I hadn't thought I'd get caught, I would have shot him dead where he stood."*

"But then neither Aaron nor Rythen would have had the fun. And I'm not sure, but I'm thinking pissing him off will cause us all a world of hurt." David snorted at him just as a man came out of the building. *"He certainly is bigger than I thought. Maybe living off the girlfriend can make you fat."*

"He was saying how she never cooks either. I guess he just has to go out all the time because of it. On her money. One of the officers asked him if he had a job, and he told him that he had no reason to work when Kim did it all." David was standing next to him when he finished. "I'm hoping that Rythen cuts him down to size. I'd do it if he did that to my mate."

"You would have already killed him." David grinned and nodded. "Come on, let's go get the piece of shit and take him to Aaron."

They walked to either side of him as he moved toward a waiting cab. When he started to enter it, David shoved his gun into his belly and told him to back up.

"I just come out of the station there, boys. If you have a beef with me, go and see them. They know what is really going on." Bradley had to hold his breath for several seconds because the man reeked of sweat and blood.

"You open your mouth again and I'll hit you because I can. I was to bring you to Aaron, but he never said how much damage we could do to you before then." Bradley jerked him to the alley behind them and shoved him against the wall. "We're here on behalf of Kim Craft. Her mate sent us."

"Her mate? She ain't got no friends that I don't have. And that ain't many. You two need to back the fuck off before I get pissed at you too. Kim ain't got the balls anyway to stand up to me, much less hire some assholes to take me down. Not that I think you can, not even the two of you old shits." Gibson laughed. "You two think you can handle me? Then bring it on, old men. I'm just itching to hurt me somebody else."

It was over almost as soon as it started. Bradley let Gibson go and he took a swing at him. David laughed and ducked another swing just as Bradley shifted. The man stood there staring at him for several seconds before he started screaming like a little girl. Bradley stood there staring as he took off running.

"Do you believe this?" David started after him but stopped and looked at him. "Go get him, big brother. I'm still laughing too hard to move. What a pussy."

The alley was a dead-end, so all he had to do was walk down it toward him. Gibson was clawing at the walls as he approached. As soon as he saw Bradley, Gibson started screaming again. Bradley had enough. Leaping at the idiot, he slammed his head against the brick wall and knocked him out. David was right, the man was a pussy.

The van pulled in just a few minutes later, and Bradley looked at his mate and driver. She smiled at him, and he had a feeling she was going to say something that would make his day even better.

"We got it." His relief was so great that he had to lean against the van before he could speak. "And we got it for a good deal less than Maddie thought too. We now are the proud owners of thirty thousand acres of land. Wanna go and pick out a mower?"

"Christ, I hope we never have to mow that. When do we take possession? Because as of last week, we needed it a month ago." She told him now. "And the houses, when can we get started on those?"

"I had the crew go out and survey the land when I heard from Maddie. She said that two of the bunk-like houses are okay to use for now, but the rest we might have to salvage what we can and rebuild." He got into the van after throwing Gibson in the back with David's help.

"We'll start on that in the morning. Aaron said he'd have some of his warriors help out. He told me that they're getting a little bored anyway." Bradley knew that wasn't true. They had been working on the newly formed forest until last night. Aaron worked his men hard.

They had done as Shamus had asked them to do, absorb the other pack into theirs. He'd had to do some serious thinking about it beforehand, but in the end it had been Elizabeth that had helped them decide.

"There are over four hundred children in the pack. Most of which will die within the first five years of being taken in by other packs. Most of them will be killed by their new alpha because, as you know, that is the way things are usually done."

"Not by me." She'd patted him on the cheek. "I see no reason to kill off our kind when there is so much we can do with our children. We need them to keep us going."

"You're a good man, Bradley. One of the best, if not the best." He'd flushed at her compliment. "But as I was saying, the young girls that are not killed for the simple reason they can do it will be auctioned off to the highest bidder so that other packs can use them as whores. And we all know what will happen to them when they've served their purpose."

They would be killed, slaughtered like cattle and then buried without so much as a headstone. He had gotten up to pace her spacious office and looked out the window that had a perfect view of the Tree of Life.

"Tell me about the tree." He had no idea why he wanted to know…probably because he had needed something to take his mind from the issue at hand. "Why does it change seasons like it does?"

"I wasn't sure what would become of the tree when I planted it. There was so much going on in my life at the time that I needed to do something that had nothing at all to do with magic. I should have known, I guess, that the entire kingdom is nothing but magic, but the little branch I put in the ground needed me. Or I should say it called to me." She had gotten up to stand next to him. "When I first planted it, I had put it in the grounds of Molavonta. And there it was a great source of bewilderment."

"How so?" When she hadn't answered him right away, he turned to look at her. "Elizabeth, what happened when you moved it here?"

"It seemed to…it came to life. It had the seasons when it was there, it changed with each solstice. But when I brought it here, it began to grow fruit." He looked at the tree, then back at her as she continued. "And it talked to me. It still does, and sometimes it tells me things I'd just as soon not know."

"How so?" She sat back at her desk and looked so sad that he wanted to take the question back. But he'd known that not talking about something that bothered you would only fester until you were sick with it. He didn't want that for her.

"I know the day it all ends. All magic. And if things done are not changed, then everything touched by magic, all of it will be no more." Bradley had had to sit down, because as much as he liked what he could do, becoming a wolf, he knew that it was only because of magic.

"What can we do?" Elizabeth looked at him and smiled. "There is something we can do, right?"

"Not on the path we're currently going we can't. A man is coming that will…he will change it all. And I don't think he is even aware of it as yet." And now Bradley knew who that man was.

"What are you thinking?" Bradley looked over at his mate and the love of his life when she pulled him from his thoughts. "I don't think I like that look. It's the one you have when you want me to do something we both know I'll hate."

"You never hate the things I want you to do to my body." She flushed and looked at David as he laughed. "But it will be something you hate. I want to retire. Soon."

"Retire? Now?" She continued to drive, and he waited for her to finish the thought that was running in her mind. "And what will this do for what is going on now? Do you think it will stop Rythen from taking away our Elizabeth? If so, then I'm all for it."

"No, but it might slow things down a bit. Let me work out some more details, and I want to talk to Aaron. Maybe we can slow this down enough where the prick has to make some decisions that are not in his little contract." Bradley thought about a strike. He wasn't sure how it would help, but if the wolves and the vampires were to suddenly stop…Bradley smiled. It might not work, but it would be fun.

~~~

Josh woke up when something cold hit him in the face. He had to blink several times to get the liquid out of his face, and a few more times to see the man standing in front of him clearly. This guy looked like he would snap him in two without a second thought.

"And you'd be correct in that thought." Josh shook his head. He'd not spoken aloud, but the man had answered him. Something was fucked up around here. Looking around, he felt his skin break out in sweat.

"Where the fuck am I?" The man didn't answer him but sat in the room's only other piece of furniture he could see. "I asked you a question, and you'd better fucking answer me or else."

"Else what? What is it you think you can do strapped to a chair in a building just far enough from other humans that no one would hear you, no matter how loudly you
~~~

screamed?" Josh felt his body grow cold. It wasn't so much what the man was saying, because that was scary enough, but how he was saying it…like he was telling Josh he'd won the lotto or something.

"Why am I here?" The guy lifted his brow at him, and Josh had a feeling he was wanting him to say please or some shit. Wasn't going to happen.

"You might be surprised at how much you'll try to please me before this is over." Josh's mind immediately went to sex, and the man laughed. "I wouldn't allow you to fuck my dog if I had one. No, I'm talking about how many things I'm going to do to your body and mind that will make you whimper at the mere mention of my name. And so you know, I've not been able to do something like this for a good long time, and I'm going to enjoy it."

"Who the fuck are you?" Fear made him snappish, but Josh knew his rights. This guy couldn't do shit to him. "What fucking reason do you have for keeping me here? I didn't do anything to you. You let me go right now."

A woman suddenly appeared behind him, and Josh tried his best not to think about how she'd done that. Instead, he tried to think of things to say to her to make her come near him. Women always did what he told them, or they'd suffer for it. It was how he rolled.

"You roll? Oh dear boy, you're going to roll all right. But I doubt very much you'll think it's a good thing." A chair appeared behind her, and she sat down. "My name is Elizabeth. This man here to my left is Aaron MacManus. I know you've never heard of either of us, but you'll remember us. Especially if things go the way we think they will. Are you willing to have a conversation with us, or do we have to resort to pain so early in our questioning?"

"I'm not saying shit. I'm not telling you again to let me—" Josh cried out when he felt something sear along his arm. He watched as a long line of his flesh opened up and blood began to pour from it. Looking at the two peels to see which of them had hurt him, he noticed that neither of them had moved. "What the fuck is going on?"

"We're torturing you." He stared at her as if she were going to next tell him that it was all his fault. "Oh, it is. We're here because of that poor girl Kim. The things you did to her have not settled well with us. And we're here to ask you to back off, or…." She shrugged.

"Back off of what? Like I told them cops, she liked it. Made her come really hard when I hit her." The growl coming from Aaron had him smile. "Piss you off does it? She fucking you too? She isn't much of a lay, is she? I mean, a woman like her should be grateful when a real man gets between her legs, but she just whined and whined about how it hurt, and that she was unsatisfied, and some shit like that."

Josh knew he was pushing the man's buttons. He had no idea why but he was really enjoying himself. He knew that they really couldn't hurt him that much. If they did, then he'd sue. He might be able to get a few hundred out of the two of them and he'd spend it on something he wanted. There was no way he was going to use it to pay off the bills like Kim was forever telling him.

Josh watched the two of them. They sat there as if this was something they did a lot of. He doubted they ever got their hands dirty, much less killed anyone. Josh started to laugh, but was cut off by Aaron.

"Would you like to know what her pain level was when you hit her?" Josh snorted. "I mean, the way you think she gets off, maybe you'd enjoy that as well."

He felt his head explode in pain and felt his nose start to bleed as the woman stood up and walked toward him. She was speaking, but he was having a hard time focusing on her words.

"You hit her in the head as soon as she walked in the door, didn't you? Then I believe you hit her in the face." His mouth felt as if he had been slapped with a ball bat, and he felt three of his teeth break in his mouth. As the woman went on about each injury he'd inflicted on Kim, he felt the corresponding pain in his body. By the time she got to him breaking his favorite bat over Kim's legs, he was dizzy sick with the pain. Aaron laughed when all he could think about was passing out.

"I'm not going to let that happen. Why should you miss a single thing when I've gone to so much trouble to let you feel it?" Aaron laughed again as he knelt in front of him to continue talking. "And now we're going to go for the surgery she had to have to put her back together. The blade they used on her belly to fix the internal damage done to her should be cutting into you about now."

Josh was begging them to allow him to die. He would take almost anything over the pain he was in, but they continued to hurt him. He had a moment of clarity when he realized that he might have hurt Kim a good deal more than he should have, but something else cut into him, and he felt his bile rise up again. He'd thrown up on himself so many times that he was covered in puke. Josh heard the other man speaking but didn't have the strength to lift his head.

"Enough." Josh was almost afraid to move. Not only had all his pain disappeared, but he was no longer covered in vomit and sweat. Lifting his head slowly, he looked up at the man who had hurt him and smiled. Josh started to speak but was cut off by a newcomer.

"I see you still think yourself above hurting women." Josh eyed this man and decided that while he was bigger than him, he didn't look like he could hurt a fly. It took him several seconds to realize that both Aaron and Elizabeth were gone.

"Where did the pieces of shit go? I have a bone to pick with them on kidnapping and causing me to hurt like they did. There was no cause for that." The man sat down and stared at him. The longer he did that, the more uncomfortable Josh felt. "You just gonna stare or you gonna take this shit off me so I can go on home? I have lawyers to call."

"I'm sure you do. But I'm trying to decide if I should kill you outright or simply take up where Aaron left off. He was very good at making you understand what you did was wrong, but I think you didn't get it. You still think it's all right to hit my mate. Or any woman for that matter." The man leaned forward in his chair and looked at him. Josh had a feeling the man was assessing him for something, but didn't know what. When he smiled, there was something very....

"You have fangs." The man nodded and laughed. "How the hell...where did you get them?"

Josh was thinking of all the hurt he could cause with a pair of those. Damn, but they looked good. He started to ask him to lean forward so he could get a better look, but the man snapped his fingers, and Josh was in pain again. This time when he threw up, he saw blood in it. Christ, he was dying, and there wasn't a goddamned thing he could do to stop it.

"Oh, you're not going die, young human, you're going to suffer. For a very, very long time if I have anything to do about it. You've touched something that belongs to me, and you'll pay for that." Pain took his breath away again when he heard the man laughing. "What you should be asking yourself about now is whether or not I bring Kim here to add her own punishment. She's become quite powerful since I gave her my blood."

Josh had no time to answer as he was split open again. This time he saw it, the way his belly was cut open and his organs still pulsed. He was terrified of puking in himself. He had no idea why he thought so, but if he did it, he'd die from it. Laughter mingled with his screams, and Josh knew there was no hope of anyone coming to save him.

CHAPTER 9

Elizabeth watched Phillip sleep. He had been resting so soundly since they'd come to their chambers that she hated to disturb him. But she really wanted him to rise. The children were coming to the house today, and she wanted to be there to see them as well. When Phillip opened his eyes and turned to her, Elizabeth felt her heart fill with her love of him.

"Do you remember the first time I saw you? You were modeling the new uniforms, and you stood there so stiff and pissed off." He nodded and ran his finger down her cheek. "I think I knew then that you were something to me, but as I had no idea what I was feeling other than annoyance toward you, I simply snapped at you."

"You wanted us to wear a suit of armor all the time. Have you any idea how hot and heavy that was?" She nodded and smiled. "And the crest was just…well, I'm very glad you changed your mind."

"You didn't like the little faerie I had put on your chest?" She laughed when he did. "It was silly. I was trying so hard to be a good leader that I simply didn't know how to let others make decisions for me."

She got up from their bed and opened the door when someone knocked on it. A small child brought in a rolling cart overflowing with flowers and their breakfast. Elizabeth sat down at the table after she left. Picking up a small flower, she took it to her nose and sniffed the scent and magic into her body.

"The swords were a better idea for a lot of reasons." She looked at Phillip as he pulled on his robe. "It showed we were strong…and it was a good deal less girly, as well."

"I know. And we so needed an army then. I remember the first fae I created. Did you know that it was Tess's great grandfather and brother who served with you?" Phillip nodded. "Creating that first couple was the best thing I could have done. Look at our Tess now. The fae are doing so much for this world and the ones beyond."

Phillip handed her a cup of tea, and she sipped it. She was thinking about her first days as queen and how many things she'd simply not understood. The rules were there, the ones that Rythen had given her to guide her, but they were, for the most part, simply too rule-like. She looked at Phillip when he cleared his throat.

"Rythen thinks I'm too soft. He believes that I have given in more than I should and that I never ruled like he had wanted me to." Phillip said nothing but sipped his own tea. "I needed their respect. And as Logan is so fond of saying, it must be earned before it can be given."

"You're thinking of the first time someone came to you with a problem, aren't you?" She nodded. "And tell me, love, what would you have done differently now that you know the complete outcome of the situation?"

The man had cut down a tree. Not just any tree but one she had only just planted in the garden. He'd been caught by the guard chopping it into smaller, more manageable pieces when they'd found him. Before he'd been brought to her, he'd nearly been hung and had been beaten within an inch of his life. His family, a wife and three small children, were all brought in as well. According to the rules in her head, when she woke, they were all to die for killing something on the kingdom's land.

His name had been Luc. His wife and three children were supposed to die by her hand, and then their bodies, small and bedraggled as they were, were to be hung from the castle walls until the birds had picked their bones clean. But Elizabeth looked at them, really looked at them before she spoke.

The man was fit, but his body looked ravaged by hunger. While his muscles were toned, his face and belly looked gaunt. He was clean, cleaner than most who worked for a living, and his clothing had been stitched over and over until it was difficult for her to tell if it wasn't more patch than original. His lady wife was no better. In fact, her clothing looked worse than his, but at least his were clean.

The children were what had her attention. All three of them stood with their parents and didn't whine or cry. The babe, only about two at the time, had watched her with eyes that looked hollow and tired. No child, she'd thought then and now, should look like that. Elizabeth had stood up and walked down the three steps to stand in front of the children.

"When was the last time you had a full meal?" They didn't answer, of course. They were raised to never speak to someone like her at all. When she looked at the mother, she pulled them closer to her as if Elizabeth would cause them harm. She'd called her guard to her, and it just happened to be Phillip.

"Take them to my kitchens and make sure they are well fed. And give them milk if we have any." The man was standing next to Phillip, and when he nodded, three more guards came forward and reached for the children. The mother stood up to her, and that was when Elizabeth realized that she was going to be a better queen than ones that simply followed the rules.

"You should not fatten them up before you kill them to make their bodies last longer on the chain." Elizabeth wanted to cry then. There had been so much hatred in her voice that she'd taken a step back. "I would rather you kill them now than give them something so kind, only to be taken from them."

"Why did you cut down the tree?" She looked at the man when he didn't answer her but kept pulling his lady wife to him. "I asked a question, and I want it answered."

"We were cold, my lady. There was no more fallen trees where we lived. The others, the ones that serve you, said that we were no longer able to have it and took it all and burned it. It seemed such a waste to me, but my family…I would do it all over again to keep them safe."

Elizabeth looked at Phillip again, and she could see the horror in his eyes. "Did you know about this? Did you know that men were wasting our resources so that others would starve?"

"No, my lady. But I will see to it they are brought before you today." She nodded and watched him walk away. She looked at the two men still there with her waiting on their next order. "Take these people home. Fill their pantry and make sure that they have meat daily."

"My lady, I would ask that you…would you mind if we shared what you give us? It would seem to be too much for one family when so many are suffering." She stood in front of him and asked him to explain. "We've been without a ruler for so long that others, men and woman who think they are fit to keep us in line, have taken over. They take and take from us until there is very little for even us to have for our sup. When our gardens fail, we are still required to give them three quarters, and it leaves us to starve. The village is…we will be no more if I cannot share what you have given us."

Elizabeth looked up when five men were brought in. They looked like they'd been well fed and were dressed in finery that made her think that these people took much more than just crops. She looked at the man, and he nodded. She moved toward the people that Phillip had brought her and smiled.

"You've been working the people and gathering some of their crops for the kingdom, I see." The first man only nodded, but another puffed out his chest.

"We have, my lady. Just for you. We had a thought that you'd need it." He looked at the family just behind her and curled his lip at them. "If we didn't need such people like them to make us rich, then I would feed them to the dogs."

She had to take several deep breaths before she could speak. This was what Rythen had wanted her to be, but she found that she couldn't do it. She could not reward these pompous asses. She realized he was speaking, so she asked him to repeat himself.

"I said that it's a good thing that you're so willing to make an example of people who do this. It will show the others that you mean business and that things will be better with you as queen." He laughed. "I had my doubts if you want to know the truth. A woman at the helm could have been terrible, but I can see that we might have judged you too harshly."

"You have no idea." She had put out her hand and killed the lot of them. When she turned to the family now cowering on the floor, she called Phillip to her side. Without taking her eyes from the small family, she spoke. "Find a group of hunters and have them take meat and whatever else they can find to the village. Make sure they all get anything they need. Also, see that there is enough wood for their fires as well as for their cook stoves. If anyone is ill, bring them back here and have my physician care for them. Why I have one is beyond me anyway."

"My lady." Phillip did what she'd said, but he never left her side. "If you wouldn't mind, my lady, might I suggest you send another group to the homes of these…creatures and have their homes ransacked? I do believe that the village could use some of what might be stored there for themselves. It's safe to assume that they will need it no longer."

When she nodded, she heard Phillip bark some other orders, and she was left with the family and him. The middle boy pulled from his mother's reach and came to her. Elizabeth knelt down to speak to him.

"You killed them." She nodded, and he looked at Phillip, then back at her. "You're our queen and you didn't kill us either. You still going to?"

"No. You were not at fault for what happened here today." He had nodded and looked at his family. "I will see to it that you will never suffer like this again. I swear to you."

He looked back at her and bestowed to her the most beautiful smile she'd ever seen. "I know that. You have a good heart like my mom. She told me once that if someone does you a good turn, you do it right back."

He had knelt before her and swore his allegiance to her. Right then and there, Elizabeth had decided that she was going to be the kind of queen this boy thought she should be.

When her assistant walked into the room, she smiled at him. "Hello, Luces. I was just thinking about you."

He smiled the same smile he'd given her all those centuries ago and bowed. "My lady and lord, the children are set to arrive at Master Aaron's house. Mistress Lizzy has gone to get them." He left her then, and she looked at Phillip.

"You know what?" He smiled and shrugged. "Rythen can go and fuck himself. I'm going to be the best I can be for whatever time I have left."

"Good for you." He stood then and reached for her hand. "My lady, shall we go and see our grandsons?"

She smiled and took his hand. It was going to be the best ten days she could squeeze out of it. Even if she had to make a few heads roll while she was at it. Laughing at her own private joke, she and Phillip went through the portal and into the kitchen of the house of Aaron.

~~~

Aaron was nervous. He wasn't sure why, but he felt…itchy. He looked up when his Sara came into the room. When she shook her head, he let out his breath he'd been holding and pulled her into his lap.

"Lizzy just called. They're having a little bit of a problem with the youngest. He thinks that he's going to be punished, then killed. She was crying when I spoke to her. Poor baby." Aaron held his mate as she cried too.
~~~

"It was what happened to his parents, if you remember what we were told. They were all gathered in a room, and they were taken away, leaving them behind. Not that I blame the courts, but the children should have been better cared for." He thought about what abuses the parents had put upon their children. "I wish they were here now. I'd like nothing more than to tear them apart myself. Staking them to the ground was too good for them."

"So Lizzy said too." When they heard their little man coming down the hall, neither of them spoke. They knew that Mathew had been told about the abuse, but they didn't talk about what they would have done had they known. When he saw them sitting in the same chair, he stopped to smile.

"Mom and Dad do that a lot. She said someday I'd have to do it too. I don't think so." Aaron laughed, and Sara made room for him to sit with them. He shook his head. "I just wanted to come and tell you that Mr. Duncan is upset with me again."

Now what? Aaron started to ask what Duncan had done now, but the look in Mathew's eyes had him stop. This was more than a broken glass or a bruised knee. This seemed very serious.

"What happened, Mathew? Did he upset you or the other way around?" Sara moved off his lap to sit beside him as they waited for Mathew to answer her. He moved to the window instead. Aaron felt the hair on his arms dance.

"I didn't mean to do it. But there was…I used my magic." They looked at each other before he continued. "He said that I couldn't have the dessert, and I was fine with that, but I thought it needed to be doubled. I know the boys are vampires, but Tristan told me they could eat stuff now."

Aaron reached for Duncan to see if he was all right. He said that he was, but his tone said that he was truly upset. *"I did not mean to yell at the young master, sire. But he startled me so. I only meant for him to leave so as he would not be covered in the…mess."*

Aaron could feel Duncan's hurt, but it wasn't directed at Mathew so much as himself. Aaron got up to move behind the young man. He could feel his pain as well, and this was directed solely at himself.

"Had you ever used it before? Your magic, had you ever used it before?" Mathew nodded but continued to stare out the window. "I see. And were you not told that your magic could only be used at the castle until you were able to control it?" Again a nod and nothing more. Aaron looked at Sara.

To be honest, Aaron was quite proud of the young man. Not because he'd used the magic, but that he'd told on himself. He was sure as he was standing there that Duncan never would have said a word about it. Aaron put his hands on Mathew's shoulders as he fought with his pride.

"You'll need to go to the kitchen and help Duncan clean up. Then when you're done, you'll go to your room and think about what harm you could have done had your magic gone astray instead of just messing up the kitchen." Mathew nodded but didn't move. "What you did was wrong, you know that, don't you?"

"I do. I could have made Duncan explode instead of just the pie he'd made." Aaron thought of Duncan making a pie and shuddered. Maybe it was a good thing that

Mathew had stepped in. "And I'll pay for the pies that Miss Sam is bringing to replace them too."

He looked up at Aaron, and the light dawned. The child knew just what he'd done. Before he could make a comment, Mathew was running out of the room. Aaron sat down hard and looked at Sara.

"He saved us all a bit of embarrassment." She nodded, smiling at him. "Good Christ, Duncan made a pie, and now we don't have to try to figure out how to eat it without being sick ourselves."

"He did. I think that we should reward him instead of…Aaron, do you think he knew what he was doing?" Aaron nodded slowly. He really did. "Oh. Oh my."

"Yeah, my thought exactly. He's a good deal more like his mother than I thought." They both laughed, knowing that even though Mathew wasn't Lizzy's blood child, he was more like her than anyone could believe. The boy was unbelievable.

When someone rang the doorbell, they went down the long staircase. Whoever this was, it wasn't family. They would have simply popped into the room.

Duncan hesitated at the door, and that was the only warning they got. As soon as he took a step back, Aaron flew to his aid just as the door opened. Sara was moving toward the kitchen where Mathew was when the man came into the house. His body was pulsing with anger, and Aaron felt his own beast rise too.

"You fucking bastard." The man moved toward him, but it took Aaron only a second to press the human back. It took him several seconds to realize that the man was related somehow to the Josh person he'd had so much fun with last evening.

"Mr. Gibson, how may I help you?" He tried his best to get away from him, but Aaron was a good deal stronger, not to mention the man was out of shape and too drunk to do more than smell up his home.

"My son. He said you and that other man you had with you beat him up. I want to show you what happens when someone messes with my boy." Aaron lifted a brow at the man, but before he could say anything, Elizabeth appeared beside him. He stepped back when she asked him to.

"You taught your boy how to knock a woman around, did you? Are you proud of the fact that he nearly killed a young woman, my child?" Aaron looked at Sara, who stood near Mathew. "He nearly killed her, and you come here to abuse my family?"

"She had it coming. Like all women do. You bitches need to learn your place." Elizabeth looked at Mathew and asked him to cover his eyes.

"If you don't mind, Grandma, I'd like to see you kick this man's butt. He really is asking for it." With a quick nod, Elizabeth turned back to Mr. Gibson.

"As you heard, my grandson said you need your butt kicked. I'm very willing to do that." He was lifted up the length of the wall and then dropped. He landed on his ass and then was lifted again. This time she stopped before dropping him. "I wish I had more time to play, but my other grandsons are on their way. You'll have to wait until later."

Mr. Gibson disappeared, and she straightened the room up before turning to them. Aaron had no idea what look he had on his face, but Elizabeth huffed at him. She glared when she spoke.

"He's in the dungeon at the castle. And before you ask, yes, I've made sure that he is cared for. Three of my most trusted maids are caring for him in ways that you might not want to know about." She moved to Mathew as Aaron tried to think what she meant. Then he decided he didn't want to know. When the doorbell rang again this time, he knew it was his daughter. She had the social worker with her or she would have come right in. Things were looking up.

CHAPTER 10

Rythen watched Kim sleep. She'd woken twice since he'd been back, but both times she'd gone right back to sleep. Aaron had told him that it was good for her to rest. But Rythen wanted her to wake so she could talk to him. He wanted to hear her voice, hear her say she was good with what they'd had to do.

They'd had to change her. It had started out as her needing to be healed, but the damage was extensive, and she was now a being much like himself. She was no longer a human in any sense of the word. Elizabeth had had to make the decision, as neither he nor Aaron was fit to do so. His pain was so great that Aaron had held him back. He'd hurt the young vampire in his rage.

"What are you doing here?" He smiled at Kim when she spoke. Finally. He looked at her when she started to sit up. "I'm way too weak for this crap. Where am I?"

"How much do you remember?" He didn't move from his chair even though he wanted to pull her into his arms and simply hold her. Rythen didn't love her, of course, but he didn't want to let her go either.

"I'd gone home and...." He knew the moment she remembered what Josh had done to her. "How long have I been here?"

"A day." She shook her head, and he moved to the edge of the bed then. "You were dying. Twice while we were trying to save you, your heart stopped beating. It was either let you die or convert you to something that would live."

"Convert me to what?" When he reached for her hand, she jerked from him. "I asked you a question. What did you convert me to?"

"To a superior being." She moved off the bed, and he watched her move about his room. Aaron thought it best that the human world didn't see what they'd done to her. He was right. She would have been too much of an oddity to them, and there was no telling what they might have done to her had they realized what she could do now.

"Elizabeth helped me change you, as did Aaron." She nodded but still moved about the room. He waited. If he spooked her, she might well hurt someone without meaning to. Her magic was untouched, and as such she wasn't used to it.

"What did you do to Josh?" He didn't want to answer that, but he really didn't have a choice in the matter. She was his mate, and he couldn't lie to her.

"He's dead." She turned then and looked at him. "I did it and would do it again if given the chance. He was…unapologetic for what he'd done."

She stared at him for so long that he began to shift on his seat. He thought she looked upset, then modified that word. She was what Aaron would call pissed. And he'd been warned that she would be.

"And because he didn't tell you he was sorry for whatever he did to you, it justified you killing him." He stood up then and moved to her. When she put her hand out, he put his over hers and held it to his chest.

"He did nothing to me personally. It was what he did to you that angered me to the point of murdering him." Kim looked at him then, and he could see her confusion and fear. "I can never harm you, Kim. Ever. What I did was because of the harm, the devastation that he did to you."

"I didn't ask you to do that." He nodded and let her go when she moved from him. He could feel her pain, not of her body because that was forever gone, but her pain of his death.

"Did you truly love him?" She shook her head and sat down on the chair near the window. "Then why do you grieve for him? Is it because he was right in saying that you enjoyed to be hurt? I cannot think that anyone would want that, but if it is your desire, then—"

"Are you insane? Who the hell in their right mind would want something like that? To be knocked around as if you were nothing more than a ball with a bat? Not me, nor anyone else I know." She looked out the window before she continued. "I'm sad because you had to kill him."

Rythen wasn't sure how to take what she said. She hurt for him killing the man…not because he was dead, but because he'd had to do it. Humans made no sense to him. He started to tell her this, but he felt Shamus laugh before he spoke.

"You'd be better off, my good man, in agreeing with her and, short of that, simply shutting up. Let her grieve for your supposed pain. I know you were probably happy to have slain the dragon for her, so to speak, but she will come around sooner if you just shut up." While he didn't understand the advice, he did shut up. She looked over at him, and he smiled.

"Can I get something to eat?" He nodded and started for the man at the door. She could have anything she wanted, even if he had to kill it himself. "I want to go home. Not to my house, but…do you know what a pizza is?"

"Pizza? No, I don't…is it a dessert?" She laughed, and he started to snap at her but was stopped again by Shamus. "Perhaps if you explained it to me, we could have one made."

Kim stood up, shaking her head. When she moved past him, he followed. The five guards in the hall had her stopping so fast that he ran into her. Rythen put his hands out to keep her from falling. He moaned when she was flush against him.

"I need for you to…please back up." He thought that he would, but he just wanted a taste of her first, and moved her hair from her neck. "Are you going to bite me again?"

"Oh yes. Many times if you would allow it." He kissed her exposed throat and then put his arms around her waist to pull her tighter against his body. "I would so enjoy doing a great many things to you. Most of which would have you screaming."

Her breathing became quick pants, and he could smell her arousal. He would have taken her right then had her belly not growled at him. Rythen kept her to his body, but he lifted his head. He would have her, but not at the expense of her health.

"This pissa thing, do you think young Aaron would know where to get one? I have heard he is very resourceful." Rythen smiled when she shivered in his arms. When she didn't pull away from him, he felt encouraged by it. Kissing her neck again, he moved back, but not before turning her around so that she fit against him.

"You're driving me nuts." He nodded, thinking she was doing the same to him. "I don't understand you at all. You run hot and cold like a faucet."

"I assure you I am very hot right now. Shall I take you back to our room and show you how hot I can make you?" She moaned, and he pulled her to him. "I would like nothing more than to strip you naked and taste all of you. Starting with your pretty pussy. I never got to run my tongue through you there. I would bet that you taste like the finest of juice."

"You have to stop this." He might have had she not wrapped her hands into his hair and rocked her hips into him. "I'm hungry."

"As am I." He lifted her up and turned to the bedroom. Food would have to wait. His need for her was too much for him to be with other people and not have her. Taking her to the bed, he took her mouth. Kissing her was quickly becoming a drug he couldn't live without.

"Please." Her clothing disappeared as he ran his mouth down to her full breast. He had no idea what she was begging him to do, but he would do it all. Taking her hard nipple into his mouth, he willed his own clothing off and felt his cock ache to be one with her. Her body arched up off the bed, and he felt her heat as she touched herself to his cock. He moved into her slowly until he was buried to his root.

"You're so hot and tight around my cock." She rolled her hips again, and he knew that his release was coming soon. "You must slow down, love. I cannot bring you pleasure if you keep this up. And I've a desire to drink from you."

Her head tilted, and he saw her pounding pulse. It wasn't what he'd had in mind, but the thought of drinking from her again was more than he could stand. Leaning into her throat, he licked along her vein and found her pulse. Biting deep, he felt her tighten around him as he drank from her. Her climax milked him, and Rythen lifted her up, tilting her so that he could go deeper within her. When she cried out again, he sealed the wound at her throat and offered her his.

"Take what is freely given. Make me yours, as I have done to you. Bite me, love, bite me when you come again, and we'll be one." Her tongue had him shivering, and before he could tell her how to do it, her teeth tore into his throat, and he cried out with it. His balls, so full seconds before, emptied deep inside of her even as she screamed out his name over and over around his throat. Rythen had had a connection with her before, but now he was as he'd told her, they were one.

~~~

Elizabeth watched the children. They were so afraid, but she knew that Lizzy and Logan would bring them around. Mathew had taken them up to his room at the mansion and shown them around, but now they sat in the chairs as if awaiting a firing squad. She looked at the oldest boy.

"You're about the same age as young Mathew here. Did you know that?" A nod. "I believe you will all have your own rooms at the house. Have you been there as yet?"

"No, ma'am." He looked at the youngest and then back at her. "Which one of us are they taking, do you know?"
~~~

Elizabeth looked at the children, then over at Lizzy. She wondered what had been said to them to make them believe that they were not staying together. When she opened her mouth to tell him what she knew, Mathew spoke first.

"My mom and dad aren't going to split you guys up. We're all going to be a family together. You guys will have a jumpstart on me what with having each other. But soon we'll have a brother or sister, and that will make us closer." He nodded, and Elizabeth wished she could remember all their names, but when Mathew spoke again, she could have kissed the boy. "Lizzy and my dad are the best in the world. And Grams here, along with Gramps, are awesome. Even Grandpa Aaron is pretty cool. He has a library that will curl your hair."

"We're never to touch stuff that don't belong to us. We've been warned." The second boy looked at the youngest and then back at them. "He won't break nothing, but if he does, then me and Peter will pay for it. He's just little yet."

"What do you think will happen to him if he does break something?" Lizzy sat on the chair next to them. Picking up the youngest, she put him onto her lap and smiled at the others while she waited for an answer.

"You don't have to beat us none." She nodded, and the oldest looked at Mathew. "The other place, they used to beat us all the time because we were different. I know we're vampires and all, but that was no reason to beat on little Kane. It's not his fault that he's a little clumsy."

"No, it's not. And for the record, I don't beat anyone." He didn't look as if he believed her, but Elizabeth watched his face. He wanted to more than anything in the world. When a vase hit the floor, she looked at Mathew, who had obviously broken it. Aaron came over, and all three of the boys cowered. Aaron looked at her and winked.

"Are you cut?" Mathew shook his head. "Well, go in the kitchen and get a broom. You broke it, you clean it up."

With that, he walked away and turned his back on them. Mathew stood up, careful of the glass, and asked the older boy if he wanted to help. And just like that the kids were best friends. When they returned from the kitchen, talking about a game that Mathew was helping Tristan with, Elizabeth looked at the younger two.

"He did that on purpose." Lizzy nodded and sat Kane on the floor so he could follow his brothers. "You told him to do that?"

"No. He asked Dad, and he told him whatever it took. There was nothing in this house that couldn't be replaced, and even if there were, family was more important." Lizzy picked up a piece of glass that had been missed, and put it in the trashcan that Mathew had brought. "They need to learn that we're not going to stake them every time they do something wrong. I have learned a lot from them concerning that other place. It wasn't as warm and fuzzy as we'd been led to believe."

Elizabeth could see that they would have a harder time with it than they'd thought, but if anyone could do it, her granddaughter could. She watched her as she helped her mom organize dinner for them all.

"I'd like to get to know them." Lizzy smiled at her and nodded. "I mean, do you think your grandda and I could have them for a day? We'd like to take them to the castle with Mathew. I'm sure it will be a nice treat for them."

"Grandmother, you know that you're welcome to take them anytime you want. And I'm sure they'd love to go with you. I can finish up their rooms while they're with you. I just found out that the clothing that they had before had been burned." Elizabeth was shocked and asked her why. "They said that they'd not been paid by the adoption agency for them, and they didn't deserve them. What they have on is all they have. And I do mean all of it. I'm going to have to go shopping on my way home from here to make sure they have pajamas to sleep in."

"I'll get them." Elizabeth stood up and reached for Phillip. They could make whatever the children needed, and Lizzy could enjoy them instead of taking them to the mall. "Tell me, do you think they'd dress in the same manner as Mathew?"

Lizzy was crying when she told her that they would. Closing her eyes, she thought of every outfit she'd ever seen Mathew wear, and put the same thing in the bedroom of each child. She varied the color and style a little, but there was no need for them to do without. She smiled at Lizzy.

"Once they touch the bags that are in their rooms, everything will fit them. I had no idea of sizes and stuff. And if they put the bags under the bed, it will give them whatever else they need as well. Clothing, that is. The rest…." Lizzy looked at her with a brow cocked much like her father would. "Oh all right, they have a great many things that you hadn't gotten them yet. I thought a nice computer would be good for each of them, and I also took the liberty of getting them a reader like Mathew has. There is no reason they shouldn't have what he does."

"No, no reason at all." Lizzy kissed her cheek. "I love you so very much. I can't stand…Grandma, has Rythen changed his mind at all?"

"No, and I doubt that he will. We've decided to live out our last days like there is nothing going on." As if she'd conjured him, Rythen and Kim suddenly appeared in the room. She could tell immediately that they were a couple, but Kim didn't look all that happy about something. Before she could try and find out what it was, Kim saw her and ran toward her. Her arms wrapped around her neck as she started to sob.

"What did you do now?" Rythen shook his head and looked as bewildered as she'd ever seen him. "She's crying, what did you do to upset her? Again."

"I didn't do anything. She said she was hungry and wanted something called a pissa. I thought Aaron could help me. I'd forgotten about the children coming. I'll take her to somewhere else. I'm so—"

"It's pizza, not pissa, you moron." Rythen simply stood there while she berated him. "Why didn't you ask someone at the castle to make her one? She could have eaten by now."

"It's not him. I swear it's not him." Kim sat up but didn't move away as she explained why she was upset. "I don't…I heard from Mr. Gibson. He said that he would find me, and I just got so upset that when I saw you, I knew you'd hug me."

"Well, of course I would." She looked at Rythen again when he moved to the other side of them on the couch. "I thought you said you'd taken care of that horrid man."

"I did. She was standing on the front steps with me, and that contraption she had in her pocket sounded. What a nasty thing that is. Blaring at you, demanding you stop everything and listen to it." She cleared her throat when he looked as if he might go off on another tangent. "I'm sorry, but we were ready to come in when that thing made a noise, and she put it to her ear. After a few seconds, she started getting upset, and by the time I was able to get it from her, she was falling apart. I didn't know what to do, so I brought her to you when she said your name."

"It's a cell phone." Mathew stood in front of her as he handed his to Rythen. "You can use it to call people."

"Why would that be able to call people to you?" Mathew shook his head and pulled his phone back. In a few seconds she saw Aaron pull his out of his pocket and answer it. He turned to them, and she realized that Mathew had called him.

"See? You can call people on it to talk to them. I know you have this great and wonderful Oz power and all, but some people, humans I guess, aren't as okay with having people talk to them through a link as we're used to doing." Mathew handed Kim a box of tissues. "Mr. Duncan wants to know if you'd like for him to order some pizzas. I wouldn't mind having a piece or two if you want him to order some."

"I'd love some pizza. And if you could see if Marco's Pies will deliver out here, I'd pay him…no, I'll have to owe him for the delivery charge." Mathew went to the kitchen again and came back just long enough to tell Kim it was on its way. Duncan came into the room with his tray of drinks a few minutes later.

"Lady Kim, I have called the shop, and they will be bringing a variety of pies to you. I do hope you don't mind, but I have also included some colas, as Master Mathew said that it is the thing to have with them." Kim nodded and smiled at him. "As for you paying for anything, that will not be necessary. The owner was quite pleased to do this for you. He is a member of my master's kiss."

"Kiss?" Duncan nodded to Kim but moved on to give out the rest of his drinks. Kim looked at Elizabeth.

"It's what a group of vampires are called. Aaron is their master." Kim looked at Aaron, who turned and winked at them. "He is a good man. A bit overbearing at times, but I've grown quite fond of him over the decades. He is nearly sixteen hundred years old."

"No way." Kim looked at the other people in the room and then at her. "And you? Are you very old? Because if you tell me you are any older than about thirty, I'm not going to believe you."

"Thank you, my dear, but I'm much, much older than that. Even more so than Aaron. By many centuries. And your Rythen is older still. He created me." She looked at her, then at Rythen.

"He said that we're mates, and that it's the same as being married. I'm not sure I want to be married to him. He's sort of…well pushy, but he's very controlling. And he killed Josh." Kim looked at the rest of the people in the room before looking back at her. "What am I?"

CHAPTER 11

Kim tried not to be overwhelmed by it all, but it was hard not to be. There were so many people there being nice to her that she wanted to tell them to back off. But she also knew that it wasn't their fault that she was feeling closed in. She looked up at Mathew, the cutest little kid she'd seen, and smiled.

"Wanna come in the game room with us?" She nodded before she could think she should probably stay put. Rythen hadn't told her she couldn't move, but she needed to and right now. She followed the boys into a room that looked to her like a miniature movie theater. She sat in one of the chairs and was handed a controller.

"We've been playing Minecraft. Have you ever heard of it?" She had but had never played. Josh played games that were more violent than she liked, but nothing she would ever enjoy playing.

"Mathew is really good about showing you, huh?" The little boy who sat next to her smiled up at her. "Have you ever seen so many nice people in one place in your whole life? And all the food? Man, I could live here forever."

She had to agree everyone was nice, and the twenty-five pizzas that had been delivered had disappeared much faster than she would have thought, but she was full now and didn't care how much it cost so long as they would let her have it again sometime. Josh had hated pizza and would never let her order it.

"You shouldn't think of him anymore." She looked at Mathew, who was showing her how to play. She started to ask him who, but he continued before she could. "The man who hurt you. I heard Grandpa telling somebody that he was well and good gone. If he is, then you've nothing to worry about. Even if he was around, none of the people here would let him hurt you again. I'd even protect you."

"I don't know what to think about that." He nodded, and she looked at the screen without seeing it. "I was a fool for staying with him. I know he would have eventually killed me. But I really had nowhere else to go."

"We didn't either." The little boy who sat in front of her looked up as he continued. "My name is Rich. My brothers are Peter, and the little one there is Kane. We was in a nasty place before Miss Lizzy and Mr. Logan came and got us. And now, we're kind of like you. Sort of a fish out of water."

She laughed and rubbed her hand over his hair and stilled. Kim felt it the moment she touched him. "You're a vampire."

"Yeah, what did you think we were?" She didn't know and told him that. "Most of the people out there are vampires, but a few of them aren't. Not many. But you don't have to worry about us biting you. Even we can tell you've been claimed, and besides we don't need to drink blood for a little while yet."

Kim had no idea what he meant, but she felt okay with it. She leaned back in her seat and watched the kids play, and even joined them after a bit. They were much better at it than she was, of course, but she'd never laughed so hard in her life. When the boys were called to head home, Kim stayed in the room for some much needed quiet time. She was almost disappointed when Rythen came in and sat down. But she was glad when he sat across the room from her.

"You've been enjoying yourself." She nodded, almost afraid of what he'd do to her for leaving the other room. "You'll have to learn to trust that none of us will hurt you. Everyone here likes you a great deal. Much more than they do me."

"Why is that?" He shrugged, and she moved on. "You're not mad because I didn't stay where you put me?"

"Why would I be mad because you did something you wanted?" She wasn't sure how to answer that, so she didn't. "Kim, are you afraid of me?"

"Yes." He looked shocked, but for some reason she didn't try to sooth it over. "You're something, I'm not sure what. You take what you want, regardless of what others around you want. You do—"

"They asked you to speak to me about Elizabeth, didn't they?" She didn't know what he was talking about and told him so. "I'm going to end her life in five days. It's our contract. I don't know what they thought you could do about it, but I assure you—"

Not being a violent person, she was just as surprised as he was when she slapped him. The need to hit him again had her doubling her fist and putting then at her sides. When he looked mad enough to hit her back, Kim raised her chin. But instead of hurting her, as she knew that he could, he took a step back.

"I'm staying here. If you're going to take away the only person who has never been anything but nice to me, then I plan to spend all the time she has left with her." She started past him only to have him grab her arm. When she stared at his grip, he finally let her go.

"You're not going to talk me out of it? You're not going to do what they asked you to do?" He laughed a bitter sharp bark of laughter, and she felt sorry for him. "I would think that you'd be the perfect person for the job. No wonder they sent you."

"You bastard." This time when she moved by him, he let her. When she started for the living room, where she knew they all were, she made a detour to the kitchen. She needed air, and there she knew she wouldn't be stopped. But she found Duncan there when she entered. He was fussing over something…she wasn't sure what…as it lay on a pan.

"I am such a horrible cook, my lady. I thought I had followed the directions, but it seems I have miscalculated somewhere." Kim thought that was an understatement. "I will have to explain to the family that I cannot do this alone."

"I can do it." She looked at him when he shook his head. "I can cook, Mr. Duncan. Very well. I just never got to because…well, I didn't get much of a chance to cook before."

Instead of waiting for his permission, she went to the recipe that he had on the counter. It was a difficult one for an experienced cook, and a novice would more than likely fail. She looked at him when he started fussing again about the smell in the room.

"Is this for dinner?" He nodded. "Well, I don't know about you, but I think this is way too much for just a few people. How about we find something fun.? I like fun, don't you?"

"Yes. It was a rare joy to have pizza brought to us. If the family wants it, we usually go and eat it there. Having it here was so much more relaxing." He went to the computer on the desk near the door and started pushing buttons. "Miss Pete has set this one up for me when she told me that the other was outmoded. I assured her that it was fine, but she insisted. This one had so many things on it I am still trying to learn."

When he got what he wanted, she stepped behind him. It was a cooking site, complete with recipes and pictures. She could see that the dinner he'd been planning said that the difficulty level was a five, and smiled. At least he had tried, something she was going to start doing right now. After ten minutes they found something they could both make and they started on it. She was elbow deep in dough for homemade bread when Lizzy and Andi, Mac's pretty wife, came in.

"You can cook?" She nodded at Andi, who sat down at the long bar. "I don't. Well, much. I find that it's a little mundane. Not to mention, messy. I must use every pot and pan in the house and borrow bowls from the neighbors to dirty up. What are we having?"

"Duncan and I thought it would be a fun night. We're making appetizers that will go with the dinner, as well as baked salmon with hollandaise sauce and new potatoes. I'm just whipping up some hot rolls." She set the bread to rest and looked to see how Duncan was doing with the small phyllo leaf cups they were going to fill with all sorts of things they'd unearthed in the refrigerator. "I've sort of invited myself to stay for a few days."

"I heard. It's why we're here." Lizzy smiled at her, and Kim had a feeling she'd been told to tell her it was time for this stupidity to stop, and for her to go home with Rythen. But she didn't. "We thought we'd come in and tell you we're shopping with Grandmother in the morning. She is wonderful to shop with. And Mom is going too."

"You want me to...I can't." She was embarrassed to say that she was broke. And even though she no longer had an apartment or a boyfriend to spend all her money, she didn't have a job. And if this thing with Rythen fell apart more, she needed a home. "I thank you, but I just can't."

Duncan pulled three glasses from the cabinet and put a large pitcher on the counter. It was the most beautiful piece of pottery she'd ever seen. After running her finger down it, all she could think about was these people had more money than she'd ever seen. She looked at Lizzy when she laughed.

"My aunt made it. She's Aric. You met her today." The wolf, "she-wolf," she'd been called. "She's very famous, and several times a year she lets us go through her studio and take what we want. Mom got this last year. I wanted it, but she beat me to it."

"Is it money?" She looked at Andi when she spoke. "Is the reason you don't want to go shopping with us, is it money?"

"I have a little, but I don't have a job." She wanted to tell them it was none of their business, but she found that she didn't want to. Kim sat down and played with her glass. "Josh wouldn't help with the bills, and I'm not sure about the ones I have now. Plus, I worked for Logan, but I don't know how that is going to work now."

"Has Rythen told you about what you get as his mate?" She shook her head at Lizzy. "He's very wealthy. More than us, I think, and we're worth billions."

Kim knew they had money, but billions? She wanted to crawl into a hole and hide. The people could buy her up without thinking about it. She started to get up to go outside when Andi spoke.

"Has he hurt you?" Kim nodded, then shook her head. "Not physically, but he has hurt your heart. I see. He is a bit of a hard-ass."

"He told me that he's going to kill Miss Elizabeth." Lizzy nodded, as did Andi. "I love her. She's like my mom. I know that sounds nuts since I've only known her for a short amount of time, but she's so wonderful. And…and he thought that you guys sent me to him to talk him out of it."

"Like you could." Kim turned to look at Lizzy when she spoke. "I figured that was what happened. He told Dad that you would be staying here for a few days and that we were to make sure you had everything you needed. Dad told him he was no longer welcome here if he'd upset you again. He and Rythen have been at each other's throats since Rythen got here."

"I don't know…what am I supposed to do with him? I mean, he's got all this…anger in him. He's almost as bad as Josh was all the time. I keep expecting him to lash out at me or hit me." She wiped at the tears. "At least with Josh I knew the rules. I don't think there are any with him."

"Have you talked with him, miss?" She looked at Duncan. "You do not strike me as a woman who would allow a man to bully her. You did so in the past, but I do believe you have gotten over that unfortunate mistake. If Lord Rythen speaks to you in a way that hurts you or says something that angers you, simply tell him. If you do not, how will he know what he is doing? I'm sure he will correct himself posthaste. He will need you much more than you him. It is the way of mates."

Kim thought about what Duncan said while the four of them finished up dinner and put it on the table. Tell him when he hurt her? She wasn't sure she was that brave. But the more she thought about it, the more she thought that she should give it a try. She wasn't sure he needed her, but then she didn't really need him either. After dinner, she spoke with Aaron.

"How do I find out where Rythen is?" He smiled a huge smile that had her seeing his fangs. For whatever reason, it didn't frighten her as much as it had before.

"Do you wish to seek him out, or simply go to where he is?" She said go to him. "Then think of him and tell yourself that you want to be there. You'll see."

Closing her eyes, she thought of Rythen and saw him. She heard Aaron tell her to will herself there, and suddenly she was standing in the room with Rythen.

"Holy hell, it worked." She looked at him when he smiled at her, and she knew this was the right thing to do. "I'm going to talk, and you're going to listen to me. Sit your ass down and keep your mouth shut unless I say you can talk. I'm sick to death of you running over me, and this will end now."

He sat and she started pacing. This was better than she'd thought. It might not make a difference, but she felt a good deal better about herself.

~~~

There were three days left, and Elizabeth was sitting alone at her tree. She came here almost daily in the beginning, and of late, she'd been less and less. She
~~~

supposed it was because she'd gotten lazy. But it was more than that. She was afraid. Now Elizabeth looked at the tree with all its seasons and felt the hot tears fall.

"I'm going to miss it here. I've talked to Shamus, and he has said that he'd put me here when the time comes. I tried to talk to Mellie, but she won't listen to me. I think she's hurting more than anyone." The faeries raced by her, and she watched as several stopped to pick up the fallen fruit from the tree. She knew that it would be in their dinner tonight, or in the basket of fruit that Shamus was forever giving to his Mellie. There was a love for the ages.

"Did I happen to mention that I've met this lovely young woman? Her name is Kim. Not Kimberly like you'd think, but simply Kim. She's a sweetheart and makes me yearn for another daughter. I don't think that's going to happen, do you?" Elizabeth laughed, and the tree shifted its branches. "I'm not as full of sorrow as I was yesterday. Yesterday, I cried at everything. Today, only about half."

She supposed it was her way to joke about things. Today was no different than yesterday, only she had one less day. As she watched Draco make his daily trip to the lake, she thought about the first dragon she'd seen. He was spectacular, and Draco was no less so as his son.

"Drake was such a man. I thought for a time he was my mate, but he was too much of a ladies' man to stand still long enough for me to figure it out. But he knew. We had such times together. I would become a dragon just to fly with him. And we'd soar over the mountains and touch our wings to the water as we sped by. He taught me a great many things about magic and humans." She thought about her first encounter with a human that didn't live on the grounds. They'd been having a picnic in the earth realm when a couple came upon them. They'd been fighting, and the woman had been crying.

"She said that she'd fallen, but both Drake and I could see that he'd hit her. The man looked as if he wanted to do so again. But I took her under my wing so to speak, and had her sit with us while Drake took the man away." She smiled. "I'm not sure what he did to the man, but I believe he was a changed man when he returned. The anger that he had was gone, and his face looked younger for it. I asked Drake what he had said to him, and he'd fobbed me off. It wasn't until years later that I looked for them again and found that they had four children, all of them boys. The woman remembered me and told me what had happened.

"'He said to him that I was with child. And that the baby would be bigger by far than him and a good deal smarter. And he would love me more than life itself.'" The woman had smiled. "My oldest is a head taller than his sire and is a good deal bigger all around. My husband has not laid a hand on me since that day. I owe both so much."

"She'd given me a cup of tea. I know that sounds so small, but it was the best I'd ever drank." Elizabeth smiled as she thought of the memory. "Okay, it was the first time I'd drank tea, but it was the best. And I've been brewing it from her recipe since then."

Elizabeth had seen many such people in her lifetime. Most of them not human, but the few that she'd encountered along the way had been special. A few at least. She thought of one such unpleasant man.

"Sherman. You remember him. He was…well for lack of a better term, he was a prick. Did you know that I'd told Mellie that he wasn't for her?" Elizabeth thought about how little she'd actually tried to tell her granddaughter, but had gone to the fade instead of staying there to help her. "He killed so many people. And hurt so many more. There were times, so many times in the beginning, that I could not believe that Mellie would listen to him. But she did, and I felt as if I was no longer needed."

It had been more than that. She'd felt as if she'd failed her granddaughter, and still did to this day. Tess had caught her thinking about it once, the way things had fallen apart because she'd been too stupid to make Mellie see reason. And Tess had a good deal to say about that.

"You think I would have met my mate? You think that Shamus would have become her mate after all this? No. He would have continued to sit on his ass, and I would have still been angry at the world. You did what needed to be done. Besides, I'm pretty sure that the Sisters Three would have turned it all around so that all of it would have happened anyway. They have a way of making things work out."

Tess had stood up when she'd said her piece and looked out over the then dead field. "Someday someone will come along and see this and say, why the hell haven't we fixed this? You know what I'll say to them? I'll say we've been waiting for you to come along and start it. We're too busy protecting the rest of the kingdom. What are you doing but sitting here on your ass and doing nothing? You've waited long enough."

Elizabeth had sat in her chair for a long moment before she threw back her head and laughed. She looked at the tree now and smiled. "There are days when I'd gladly strangle the girl. What do you suppose she'd say to me today? I'm betting it would be to get up again. She won't be able to do it all on her own."

Moving toward the living field, she thought of all the magic that had been given to Rythen to do this. She also wondered if he knew that had all of the vampires in Aaron's kiss and every wolf in Bradley's pack not pushed him at the last minute that it would never have been as far along as it was.

"I suppose the arrogant ass thinks he did this all on his own. Well, I have news for him. He's going to learn what it's like to have your power sucked right from you. As of today."

CHAPTER 12

"We've been given the okay." Aaron looked up from his computer when Bradley flopped down in the chair across from his desk. "Elizabeth called on me an hour ago and asked if what we had planned would really work."

"Do you think it will?" Bradley shrugged, and Aaron leaned back in his chair. "You really don't know or you're afraid to commit?"

"If everyone in my pack stopped shifting, and you don't do whatever it is you do, then I'm thinking it will put a big dent in the magic they all have. We both know that our magic is more powerful when they are around. What if the reverse is true? That they need us much more than we need them."

"I don't have magic." Aaron no longer believed this, but he'd been saying it for years, so that now it was as if it were a requirement to do so. And Bradley, like he knew he would, rose to the bait.

"How the hell after all these centuries can you still believe that? Christ man, you live with a woman that has so much in her body that plants grow faster when she simply walks by them." Aaron laughed, and Bradley calmed down. "You drive me nuts, have I told you that lately?"

"You have, and I love you too." The rest of the morning consisted of them gathering the other leaders in the area and telling them the plan. It still amazed Aaron how many people loved him. He knew that each and every one of them would do whatever he would ask of them regardless of any harm to them. Colin sat back when they had finished the plan.

"You think a day will be enough?" Aaron nodded. "It's going to be hard on the younger vamps, but we'll make it work for them too. No magic, huh, and no shifting either? We can make a difference. If not, we might have to start a war to feed us all when it's over."

"I don't think it will come to all that." Colin looked at Bradley when he spoke. He eyed him in a way that Aaron knew that whatever Colon said next was going to piss the wolf off.

"You gonna turn over your virgins to us for food when we come knocking, man? I hear that you have a few of them in your own household. Nine daughters and counting last I heard."

"You stay away from my daughters and I won't have to tear your throat out." They all laughed, but each knew that if anyone came near any of their families to cause harm, they would gather together like the war that Colin mentioned and kill whoever dared touch what was theirs.

It was set. Tonight, when the sun went down, every paranormal they knew and some they did not would not use magic. Aaron wasn't really sure how much it would affect the castle, but he was willing to bet it would be something. As the rest of them went to their homes, he started for his lair and heard loud voices in the kitchen. He went there to see what was going on.

"What do you mean you are going to get this thing between us taken away? You cannot do that. I forbid it." Rythen would have to learn to take that word out of his vocabulary if he ever thought to have his mate treasure him. Right now she looked as if she wanted to stuff him in a treasure chest and bury him deep in the ocean.

"You can't forbid me to do anything, you childish ass. Where do you get these insane rules of yours? No one in their right mind thinks like that anymore." Kim huffed at him as she sat down and continued snapping the green beans on the bar. "I tried to tell you yesterday and you wouldn't listen. I'm finished trying to talk to a person who is ten times the most stubborn man I've ever met. You, sir, are dismissed."

"Dismissed? What the hell does that mean?" Kim didn't even look at him as Rythen started pacing the room. "If you want to know stubborn, you should look in the mirror. You are the queen of it. All I said was for you not do kitchen work. Why does everything I say to you have to be met with anger?"

"Because you never ask, you demand. I'm sick to death of men demanding crap of me. I'm a person." She looked up at him when he opened his mouth to speak. "And I swear to you if the next words out of your mouth are not 'I'm sorry,' I will have someone put a hex on your dick."

"My dick. Why is it that every woman I meet wants to do something to that part of my body?" Aaron heard Kim mumble and nearly lost it when Rythen asked her to repeat herself.

"I said it's because that is where your tiny brain is. It's the only thing you seem to ever know how to use." Aaron cleared his throat so they'd see him, and they both looked toward him. Kim flushed a bright red when he winked at her.

"I couldn't help but overhear you. I'm reasonably sure the neighbors were able to overhear you now that I think of it." He sat down across from Kim. "Do you know where Duncan and my wife have gone?"

"Duncan had an appointment, and Mrs. Mac said she had to go and gather the troops. I think it has to do with the fact that I'm not going shopping with them, but I'm not sure." Aaron looked at Rythen when Kim did. "He seems to think that he'll pay for everything I want, and I think I should earn it."

"As you should." Rythen growled, but Aaron ignored him. "I'm not sure why he's here. I think I told him never to return. But that's not what matters. I should like to give you some money."

Before she could protest, which he was sure she would, he raised his hand. Rythen was not put off. He blustered about his mate this and that, and Aaron snapped his fingers, sending Rythen to the castle.

"You can't give me money. Though I'd be glad to pay you if you showed me how to do that trick." Aaron felt his anger for this woman soar. She'd been told nothing of what she could do or how to do it. And Rythen had been ordering her around. Much like he'd done to Sara all those decades ago.

"You've been cooking for us. And if I don't miss my bet, having a good time at it. And Duncan said he is learning a great deal about cooking from you." She nodded and smiled. "He told me about the measuring cups. I nearly had to leave the room. There are times when I swear that he sits in here making things up just to see if he can make me laugh."

"He's a wonderfully naive little man, and I adore him. And the measuring cups. That was…he actually thought that he could use any cup and it would do. Some of the mugs you have in your cabinets are quite large. He said that Aric made them." Aaron nodded. They had a great deal of her things. "And the measuring spoons too. I nearly fell off my chair when he told me that he thought the capital 't' was for a serving spoon and the smaller one for anything else. Poor man. How long has he been working the kitchen for you?"

"Since well before I can remember. Either of us, for that matter. I think someone told you how old I was." She nodded. "With my age comes great knowledge. Not all of it relevant, but most of it. And I'll tell you now that I was no different than Rythen when I met my Sara."

"I don't believe it. You love her so much, and it shows in everything you do with each other. I'm…well, it's very heartening to know that there are men like you out there. Mac is much like you and Mr. Wolff. He and his wife are amazing together."

"I once told Sara she'd beg me to beat her butt." Kim laughed as he'd hoped she would, but he assured her it was true. "We were so mismatched, I thought. And because of my ignorance, I nearly lost her. And my children. Because without her, there would be no kiss, and I'd have died without her."

"I doubt Rythen would allow death to take him. He's so stubborn." Aaron didn't point out that she seemed to be holding her own in that department, but only nodded. "He's going to murder Elizabeth, and he thinks that I'm going to somehow try to talk him out of it. I want to, with all my heart I want to, but I know that he'll do it anyway, and I'll be hurt by it."

"He claims that because he has a contract that it makes it unbreakable. I think he's just afraid if he doesn't follow through on this, people will believe him a failure somehow." She snorted, and Aaron laughed. "Men have done stupider things in the name of a good contract."

"So he's going to kill her simply because it's written down?" Aaron nodded. "I suppose you have a plan to make sure that doesn't happen. I'd like to help if I can. I love her so much."

"You cannot, my dear. One of the things about being a mate to someone is that you cannot harm them or be harmed by them. And this will hurt you in ways I can't explain." She nodded. "But as for me giving you your wage. You've done a fantastic job for my household, and the boys said they've never eaten better. So for this I will give you what I consider a good wage."

Money appeared between them, and she didn't touch it. He knew it was a great deal of money. Though he had no use for it really, he knew the value. And giving her ten thousand dollars was way overboard. But he liked her and wanted to piss off Rythen a little more.

"He won't like this." Aaron said nothing. "I'm going to take it for that reason alone. But it's more than I would earn in six months at my old job." The phone ringing gave him no opportunity to answer her. She got up to answer it just as Duncan and Sara came into the house. He was kissing Sara when he heard Kim cry.

"I told you to leave me alone. I didn't have anything to do with the death of your son. And to be honest with you, I think he got just what he deserved." He moved up behind her and put his ear to the phone. The man on the other end was spewing all sorts of comments and nasty things to Kim when Sara appeared in front of them.

"Hang up." Kim held the phone to her ear and stared at Sara when she repeated herself. "Hang up, love. Nothing he says to you will matter in about five minutes. Because I'm going to kick his ass myself."

Kim put the phone on the cradle and wrapped her arms around Sara. As she cried, Aaron turned to Duncan. The man looked as if he had been hurt by the words too. When Aaron said his name twice, he looked at him.

"Call Elizabeth and Mel. Tell them what's going on. Have Pete change out the number here and make sure that that call is traced." Duncan nodded. "And make sure that Rythen is made aware that his mate is being threatened."

"I will, sire, but you should know that I had Miss Pete put a device on this phone yesterday. I had Lady Kim give the number to that horrid man so that we may track his behind." Aaron hugged the man to him. "Well, sir, had I known how happy that would make you I would have done it sooner. You look, if you do not mind my saying so, as if you have swallowed the robin."

"Canary, and yes, I think I might have." Aaron went to his lair knowing that as soon as he woke, things were going to be hot. Laughing, he contacted Bradley and asked him to double the guard around the estate.

"Done, and Pete said to tell you that she's got him, whatever that means. She also said to tell you that you're to stay out of this. Kim and the women are going to take care of this. She said Kimmy needs it."

Aaron agreed. She did need this, and Aaron nearly skipped to his bed. Yes, sir, things were about to take a very nice turn.

~~~

Rythen wanted to smash something. Or kill someone. He'd never been so angry in his life. And considering his
~~~

age, he was doubly angry. He paced the room several times before he came up short. He'd never heard Elizabeth enter. She sat down and asked him to have a seat as well.

"What's happened?" She only patted the seat, and he wanted to refuse her but knew that if he didn't do as she said, he'd never hear what she had to tell him. "I don't think I like this new you. I would very much like it if you were to go back to the way I made you."

"Too bad. Now, I need for you to remain calm when I speak to you." He nearly left her to find someone who would give him the answer correctly, but three guards walked in fully armed, and he sat back down. "Are you going to behave or do I need to have them hold you?"

"I want you to know that I'm not at all happy with the way things are going here, and I'm sick to death of being treated like an infant. I'm a grown man, you know."

"Then I would propose you start acting like one." She sat there for several seconds waiting for him to answer. He nodded once, and she started talking. "Kim has been threatened by the father of the man you killed. Aaron said that he told her he was going to get her and make her pay like his son should have. Aaron also said that he has a plan."

"And this plan, do I get to help my mate or has that right been taken from me as well?" He flushed when he thought about what he'd said. In the past hour since Aaron had sent him here, he'd been doing a lot of thinking. "I've been somewhat overbearing to her."

"Somewhat? From what I've heard you've been no less a bully than the man you killed. She told us that at least with Josh, she knew the rules. If she messed up she'd get hit. With you it's not the same." Rythen stood up and started to pace, but one of the guards drew their sword, and he sat down. While they wouldn't be able to kill him, they would hurt him. And of late, he wasn't so sure they wouldn't be able to kill him. Things were not the same as when he'd left them.

"She's nothing like I thought a mate would be." She was more, but he wasn't going to tell Elizabeth that. Her head was too full now of what he'd done wrong about his mate. "She told me last night that if she wanted to, she could go to the Fates and have them take this away from us. What right does she have to even think those sorts of things? Is her life not for the better?"

"I would say it's not." He looked at Elizabeth when she spoke. "What does she know about herself? Nothing. Does she have a home? A place to call her own? Nope. Does she have any idea what she is? She's asked that of several people, and none of us know just how to answer her. Telling her she is everything only gives her more questions to ask. She wanted to go shopping with us today. Did you know that she refused? Now ask me why?"

"Aaron had said she had no money. He said he was going to give her some. He had no right to do that. I have plenty of money if she wanted to buy several stores. She needed only to ask for it." He looked at her when she snorted. "That is a nasty habit you have. What does it mean?"

"It means that you're full of shit. And why should she have to beg you for money as if she were a beggar? Should you not have provided her with all she wanted or needed? Did you know that she has no clothing? Not a stitch. This morning Sara lent her a blouse to wear. There is no telling what she is doing for underclothing." The thought of her underclothing made him shift on his seat. He wanted her, and she'd refused him twice now.

"She is making this harder on herself than she needs to. Why doesn't she just listen to me? I will make her life perfect." Elizabeth laughed, and he decided that he was going to never talk to her again. Then he was brought up short, knowing that in a few days he never would. For the first time in all this, he thought about her as his friend.

"Kim is being threatened, and she is going to take care of it on her own. And when she does, what do you think she'll think about you and your rules then?" He knew what she thought now, and was afraid of what might happen if she could prove to herself that she didn't really need him.

"I have been a fool." Elizabeth nodded. "Well, you could have given me a second or two before you agreed with me. I don't know what I'm doing."

"No, you don't. And you're going to lose more than a mate if you don't figure it out." He knew that too. Once Elizabeth was gone, he'd have to stay for a time, as it was written, but he had a feeling he wouldn't be welcome anywhere if he did. Not even with his mate. She would be well cared for, but not by him.

"I would ask that you help me." She nodded. "I'm…I need to earn her trust and her love. I don't love her now, but I do…she is a spitfire, is she not? How did I miss that when I first met her?"

"You were too busy making demands. And I cannot help you." He started to protest, but she cut him off. "I'm going to spend my last days with my family, and you are not included. You might have been at one time, but I, like your mate, cannot stand you."

Shamus appeared a few minutes after Elizabeth left. He had been thinking about what he'd been doing and looked at the proud king sitting before him.

"I think in order to understand my own mate, I have to understand Elizabeth." Shamus leaned back on the couch as he got up to pace. "I'm not very good at women, as you might have guessed, and since she is the only female that I actually know, mayhap you should tell me what you know about her."

"She is the greatest woman I know. And she has a heart of the purest gold. Elizabeth will support you in ways you cannot believe, even if it's to let you fail, but she will be there to pick you up when you do. She'll dust you off and show you how to start again." Shamus smiled. "What do you want to know?"

"Everything." Shamus nodded and started talking. Rythen wasn't at all surprised by the amount of respect and love he heard from the younger man. But he was surprised by how much she did daily to keep them all together.

CHAPTER 13

To say she was afraid would have been funny. Kim was terrified. And not only that, she was sure that she was going to die. She felt someone move across her mind like a soft touch and waited, tense.

"You're not going to die. Why would you even think that? Didn't I show you how to do some pretty awesome stuff? And your sword work is pretty fucking amazing too." Kim smiled at Tess. The woman was like this amazon on steroids. "Thank you."

"I don't know why I let you talk me into this. He's going to come in here with guns blazing, and I'm going to end up a puddle on the floor." She looked around. "You know if I do live through this, I think I'd like to buy this building."

"Why is that?" She thought it was Lizzy this time, and she told her it was. "What would you do with this building that makes you think of that now?"

"I can see a bunch of shops in it. You know, like an open air market. And artistic people selling their wares on pretty little carts. Like in New Orleans, but more…I was going to say artsy, but that's not it." She tried to think. "You know…have people doing what Aric does, making their stuff and selling it. I don't know how a potter would do it, but you think people would come to see her throwing pots, don't you?"

She felt foolish and nearly told them to forget it, but Andi spoke up. "I know this woman who does the most amazing knitted things. Little Dunc has two of her hats, and he had a bunch of her little booties. She'd make a killing at something like that."

"You'd have to make the rent affordable," Lizzy said. "Most people who are just starting out have very little money. And maybe you could provide them with some stuff to make it work. Like a cash register and some shelves." Kim found herself getting into this too. She could see it coming together and spoke up when Lizzy told her about a man she knew who made jewelry.

"And in the summer, a garden could be made so that visitors could come and have a seat, maybe even enjoy an ice cream or a hot dog." Lizzy laughed, but she didn't feel foolish. It was just a dream, but it kept her from being scared for a few minutes. The door opening just beyond her had her freezing up, but Tess told her to be calm.

Tess had shown up just as they were leaving the house. Kim had a feeling she'd been asked to go with them, and after she'd taken her into the yard to work on a little self-defense, she was sure of it. But she was glad for the fae. Kim had to smile. A fae…she knew, a flipping fae person.

"Well, you showed up, didn't you? Didn't think you would with all this shit going down about my son being abusive to you. I think you should know that nobody else complained when they was with him." She looked at Mr. Gibson and decided that the man was hurting. "He wasn't doing nothing you din't want."

Okay, maybe he was just as asshole. She stiffened her spine and took a step toward him. Tess had told her that bullies usually didn't like it when their intended victim did that. He frowned at her and took a half step back.

"Your son was an abusive ass, and I'm beginning to think you taught him everything he did." The man nodded, clearly confused by her statement. "Do you know what he did to me? How badly he'd hit me sometimes?"

"Well yeah. Duh? Why, if you're going to hit someone, would you be gentle about it? Women only should have one position, and that's flat on their backs. Whether they're there because you knocked them there or they're servicing you, that's where they should remain."

Her laughter bubbled up before she could stop it. She had no idea why she thought it was so funny that he'd think this way, but it had her nearly doubling over with it. When he took a step toward her, she stood up and faced him. He drew back his hand to hit her, and she spoke.

"You do and it will be the last thing you ever do in your short and miserable life." Her voice surprised her at how calm it was when inside, she was terrified beyond her next breath. "I will not allow a man to touch me again in violence."

"You think you're so tough? I got news for you. I've hit more women in my lifetime than most men fuck." He did a small lunge at her, and she stood her ground. "You're nothing to me. And when you're dead and in the ground, nobody will give a shit about the woman who murdered my son."

"But they'll know your son, won't they? They'll know that his entire life he was abused by you and your wife. That the two of you would lock him in a cage not even big enough for a small animal. But you treated him that way, didn't you? Locked him in there to teach him a lesson he never forgot." Kim had no idea why she was getting these thoughts, but knew that it wasn't from the women with her. "What about all the times you would send him out into the cold, when all he wanted was something to eat? If anyone is at fault for your son's death, it lays solely at your doorstep."

"You don't know what you're talking about." He started for her again, and she kicked him in the shin, bringing him to his knees. "You're going to pay for that, bitch. You just wait and see."

"Try me." He looked up at her as he stayed where he'd fallen. "Get up off your lazy fucking ass and make me pay. Or are you too afraid of me? Is that it? A woman fights back and you're suddenly not going to play? Get up."

"You're nuts." She reached for his arm to pull him up. She'd had enough of this. But his next words had her still. "I'm going to kill you when you least expect it. Not now, because you probably got this place all wired up. But I'll get you."

Kim put her hand on his head. Her intention was to knock him all the way to the floor, but the moment she touched him, she felt a hard current run up her arm and to his head. And in what seemed like hours but had to have been only seconds, she pushed as much of herself into him as she could before someone else touched her. She looked up into Elizabeth's face, and felt as if she'd been given a great gift in their friendship.

"Let him go. Kim, honey, let him go." She felt her finger let him go and her body grow weak from it. "That's my girl. Just lay down here."

Her body was being laid down, and she couldn't find the strength to argue. When someone else stood over her, she looked up into the grinning face of Lizzy. She saw Andi there as well.

"Did I kill him?" Lizzy shook her head and they both moved so that she could see him. He was lying on the concrete floor sucking his thumb and sobbing like a baby. She looked at Elizabeth, not understanding. "What happened to him?"

"You gave him what he'd been giving every woman he'd ever met, as well as the pain that his son suffered at his hand. You gave as good as you got."

The police were called, and Tess talked to them. Kim didn't understand why they weren't slightly freaked out by her appearance when Lizzy walked up to her and wrapped her arm around her shoulders. She asked the beautiful woman why they weren't freaked out.

"They don't see her like we do because she doesn't want them too. You should see yourself as we do. You glow." Kim shook her head. "Yeah, you do. And there are all kinds of beautiful sparks coming off you all the time. It's your magic. It's powerful."

"I have no idea what you're talking about." Andi walked up to them, and when Lizzy told her what they were talking about, she pulled her along to a closed door. When she opened it, Kim looked at the woman staring back at her in the mirror.

"How...how did this happen?" Neither one of them answered her, but Kim didn't care. The girl looking back at her seemed to be something out of a faery tale. Kim looked at Tess when she came up behind her. Then Lizzy and Andi were talking to Elizabeth as Mr. Gibson was being loaded in an ambulance.

"You okay?" She nodded. Tess grinned. "As you might have guessed, I came along because I was asked to do so. Rythen sent me…well, he asked me if I'd make sure you were okay. I think I'll be happy to report that you did better than okay. You fucking rocked the house."

"Do you know how long he's going to be like he is?" Tess told her forever. "I didn't mean to hurt him like that. I only meant to keep him from hitting me. Why didn't Elizabeth pull me away sooner? And now that I think about it, when did she show up?"

"I can't touch you." Kim frowned. "You're royalty, yeah, but you're a powerful being and I can't touch you without your permission or you're going to cause harm to another member of the royal family, like Sara and her family or Queenie and hers. You did neither, and I had to call someone who could."

"What about Lizzy or Andi, aren't they royalty too? Not that I believe that I am, but wouldn't they have been able to pull me away from him before I hurt him that badly?" Tess shrugged and smiled. Kim looked at the two women that turned when she did, and it hit her. "They're going to have a child, each of them."

"They are. I don't know if Andi is aware of it yet, but Lizzy knows. Can you tell what they're having too? You should be able to." Kim reached out to them and knew that Lizzy was having a son and that Andi was having twins. One of each. "You're getting really good at this. What am I having?"

"A son." Tess nodded and smiled at her. "And had Aaron known or even any of the rest of them, you wouldn't have been able to come here."

"They're very protective of their women." Kim had seen that. "There's something else you should know. I'm probably not supposed to tell you this, but Rythen is taking mate lessons from Shamus."

"Mate lessons? What the hell are those?" When Tess laughed, Kim had a feeling she didn't want to know. But as she moved closer to the other women it occurred to her. He was learning to deal with her.

"Not deal with you, but to be a better man for you."

She felt Rythen touch her as if he were standing next to her. *"You are not harmed, are you?"*

"No. He never touched me." She wanted to not speak to him, but she was very proud of herself today. She hadn't crumbled under the pressure. "I took care of myself. I won't let another man harm me again."

"And I did." She didn't answer him because they both knew that he had. *"I'm trying to do better. I've been somewhat…I've been a pain in your ass. As it has been pointed out to me a great deal."*

"You're not going to hear me say anything different." He laughed, and she felt her heart take an unexpected twist. "I'm not going back there with you. I want to be here, with my friends. You aren't right now."

"I realize that. And I'm sorrier than you'll ever know about that. I'm going to make it up to you. I swear." She didn't say anything, but he continued anyway. *"I would very much like to take you out to dinner tonight. I understand you'll be in town with the others. I could meet you somewhere."*

"I don't know. I've never been…the only out to dinner I know is a fast food place. What did you have in mind?" She waited for him to answer her as she climbed into the limo with Lizzy and Andi. Elizabeth and Sara, along with a couple of the other women that Sara knew, were going to meet them downtown.

"I have in mind a very elegant place where it would pale in comparison to you." She flushed, and Lizzy winked at her. *"Ask one of the women to help you find something lovely to wear, and I will take care of the rest. I'll meet you at the riverfront at six."*

She told him that would be fine and felt the connection close. She looked over at Andi and started to ask her about a dress when she spoke first.

"You should do it." She frowned, wondering how she knew about the dress when she continued. "The shops. You should do it. I'll help. I know the person who owns the building, and I'm sure he'll give you a good buy. Black owns it, Lizzy's family business."

"I was just telling him about your idea, and he loves it. He said if you want to rent it or buy it, he's in." Kim started to shake her head when they both continued talking at the same time. They had the entire building set up and tenants practically in it before they got to the first shop. She was almost too excited to tell them she didn't have any idea how to make this work, much less the money to do it. The rest of the early afternoon and well into dusk was a flurry of shopping and food. But most of it was friendly talk. And Kim learned a great deal about what she was.

~~~

Rythen was terrified nearly out of his boots. He'd been told all day that if he'd just learn to listen rather than speak, he'd find his mate would like him. He had no idea how that was supposed to work. And when he saw her at the corner where he'd asked her to meet him, he nearly swallowed his tongue. Christ, she was a goddess.

He moved toward her slowly, wanting to absorb as much of her beauty as he could. There was so much of her
~~~

to see that he wanted to wrap her up in a blanket and take her home to peel her open. When she turned and saw him, he whimpered when she smiled. A man could only take so much.

He wanted to tell her how beautiful she looked. Rythen had practiced all day what to say to her, what to compliment her on, but as soon as he was close enough to touch her, he could only think of one thing. He had to touch her. Pulling her into his arms, she went willingly. And when his mouth touched hers, he knew that for as long as he was allowed to have her, this would be the best moment of his life.

"You're simply beautiful." Her cheeks glowed with her embarrassment, and he found that endearing. He was glad now that he'd let Shamus talk him into this. And now he had to make it through the night by wooing her and making her like him. He knew that he could do it.

"Are you hungry?" When she asked him that, he thought of the first time they'd said that. And he'd been hungry then, but nothing compared to how hungry he was for her now. But taking a step back, he took her hand, and after a brief kiss, put it on his arm. He was taking her out, and they were going to have fun.

"I had to ask around about this place. Duncan showed me how to look things up. Then I had to have Pete show me how not to do it." Kim laughed, and Rythen wanted to hear her do it again and again. "He does have a knack for confusing one, doesn't he?"

"I think he's charming. I had so much fun helping him out in the kitchen. He's very lacking in that part of the house, but he runs a tight ship elsewhere." They were taken to their table by a very nice young man, and Rythen realized he was a faerie. When they were alone again, he asked her if she had caught that.

"I did. I'm not perfect at it yet, but Tess showed me how to tell what was what. I still get the cats messed up, but Lizzy assured me that it would come with time." He nodded, grateful for the women of Aaron's kiss. He'd been terribly lacking in her training, and he….

"What did you say?" He leaned closer and realized his mistake at once. Her scent called to him, and he wanted her right now. Pulling her toward him, he settled her over his lap and took her mouth before she could tell him no.

"We're going to get thrown out." He thought he answered her statement but really didn't care. As soon as he pulled the shadows around them, he was going to take her, and damn the people in the room with them.

"I need to be inside of you." She nodded and sat up on her knees. He nearly cried out when she reached for his cock. Her fingers were sliding down his front when he felt the slightest bit of magic shift.

Rythen lifted her dress up over her hips and saw that beneath the incredibly lovely silk creation, she wore thigh high stockings. Running his hand around to her pussy, he moaned when he was able to slide into her without any interference. The cool breeze over his cock was all the warning he had that she'd freed him. She lowered herself over him so that he was buried to the root. Neither of them moved.

The next time he felt the magic shift, someone looked at them. It startled him a little that anyone could see them with his magic so tight around them, but Kim rolled her hips, and he forgot everything. She moved slowly, back and forth, until he thought he might explode any second.

Rythen untied the top of her dress to expose her full bare breasts.

Her nipples were hard and thick. Taking the tip into his mouth, he bit down hard enough to have her cry out, but not hard enough to draw blood. He wanted to suckle from her here and would as soon as he made her come. Gripping her hips to speed her movements up, he was startled when someone screamed. Looking around the room, he could see that everyone was staring at them.

"What's going on?" He didn't know and tried again to pull the magic around him. It simply wasn't there. Nothing was. Pulling Kim closer to his body, he tried his best to shield her from the fifty or so people in the room with them, but they'd seen enough to know that they'd been having sex. The man that had spied them first was taking pictures with his phone. Rythen growled.

"Get out." No one moved, and Rythen felt his beast, never far from the surface anyway, let go. Rythen shoved Kim aside and rushed the man, only to be brought up short when someone hit him from behind.

His arm was being pulled, and he turned to hit the person when he realized suddenly it was Kim. She was pulling her clothes back on her body even as she rushed them to the door. His pants, now down around his ankles, nearly tripped him up twice, but he just managed to keep going until they were outside. They made their way to the alley directly behind the restaurant just as the police pulled in front. He had to get them home before anyone found them. Rythen looked at Kim to see if she was all right and took a step from her when he saw that she'd been clawed.

"It's fine." But it wasn't, and they both knew it. Her cheek was now marked with three very deep cuts that he'd done. His beast had hurt her. "I want to go home. Just…let's just leave here before someone else takes a picture and I can't get the phone."

He watched her drop the one the man had had and crush it under her heel. When he reached for her, she took a step back, and he felt his heart tear open. Rythen had no idea what had happened in there, but he would before the night was out. When he tried to summon someone to come and get them, he knew real fear. His magic was gone.

"Can you use your powers?" She shook her head. Handing her his handkerchief, he watched as it filled with blood. "I'm so sorry I hurt you, love. I never meant to harm you."

"It wasn't your fault. You were…I'm not sure what you were. You kinda scared me too." He nodded and straightened his clothing. They had to get home, and the sooner the better. But where was home? He suddenly realized he had no idea where to take her so she would be safe.

"I need to get us a place to stay. Do you know of a home or a vacant building?" She shook her head, and he had a moment of panic when she staggered slightly. Rythen picked her up and reached for Logan.

"I'm not going to help you." Rythen stopped moving when Logan spoke before he could ask him for help. *"I'll bring Kim here, but you will have to fend for yourself."*

"You know what happened to us?" Logan said he did. *"Then I demand that you explain to me what happened. My mate is hurt and whatever you did was the cause of it."*

"They stopped using magic." Rythen had been moving toward a row of cars when what Logan said had him stop.

"I had no idea it would drain you so badly, but I guess when the power of many stops supporting you, it can have major effects."

"You're saying that no one is using any magic?" Logan told him that Aaron's kiss as well as the pack had decided to never use it again. *"That's not possible. How will they shift? How will Aaron and his family feed? Tell them I said to stop this nonsense immediately and use their magic that I gave to them."*

"I'm pretty sure that they could care less. And you might want to get used to not having it too. Once Elizabeth is gone, they said that you're going to be fucked." And they would be as well.

"They're just being childish. My mate was hurt by this stupidity, and now you're telling me that they'll hold their magic hostage until I say she can live?" He laughed bitterly. *"Well, I won't have it. She will die no matter what they think to do to me. And when they are starved and their own bodies begin to betray them, I shall tell them it was all for naught."*

"I think you should think this through, Rythen. Even if I do find a way to stop this, you're still going to have to live with these people. And if you decide to fuck it up with Kim, which I'm betting you're on the road to doing now, she'll have to stay with one of them. What do you suppose will happen to her once you're gone?"

"Gone? Gone where?" He hadn't talked to Kim as yet, but he had already made arrangements for her to join him in a faerie ring. They'd live out their days until he had to return in bliss and quietness. He glanced at her as he put her into the first car he found with the doors unlocked. His heart twisted again.

"She can't go with you. I forbid it." Rythen stood up so quickly that he knocked his head on the top of the car door. *"And you'll have to learn to live with disappointment on that one. She's not going to the fade with you."*

"And how will you stop me?" Logan laughed, and Rythen felt his temper rise almost out of control. *"You will blackmail me, too?"*

"No. I don't need to. You didn't change her with permission. She belongs to me until such time as I release her. Read the laws you wrote. You'll see that I'm correct." Rythen didn't need to. He knew that Logan was right. But he had to get her somewhere safe so he could look into what the magic was doing…or the lack of it. Things were going bad, and he needed somewhere to think. And he couldn't go to the castle, so he was well and truly fucked, as he'd heard Aaron said on occasion.

CHAPTER 14

Logan watched Rythen pace. The man was pissed, and for good reason. Aaron was a good deal more powerful than Logan had realized, as was the alpha. Bradley had been able to call his men in and make them do just what he'd wanted without having to give any order. It made Logan want to talk to him about ruling. Aaron, too, for that matter.

"When will they stop this nonsense?" Logan looked at Aaron, who had yet to say a word. This had been two hours ago. A car had been sent for them, and when they'd been brought to his house, Aaron had come when he'd asked him. Logan wondered now why he'd called him. He looked at Rythen when it looked as though Aaron wasn't going to speak.

"I'm not really sure what you think they've done to you." Rythen sputtered for a few seconds before Logan continued. "I'm reasonably sure that there is no law that says they have to use their magic. And if that affects you in some way…well, I will say I'm glad for it."

"You're siding with him." Rythen pointed at Aaron as he continued. "You think this is going to endear me to you or something? You may be the Keeper of Secrets, my good man, but that does not keep you from my wrath. You'll call them off or I shall take matters into my own hands."

"Like what? You'll take her last day away?" They both, he and Rythen, looked at Aaron when he spoke finally. "You can't do that. You see, I've read the contract myself. It has a specific time as well as a date that you signed her life away. And if you deviate from that at all, even for a second, things will be null and void. Perhaps I should let you. Then everything will go back to normal and you'll go back to wherever it is you were hatched from."

"Why you—" Logan stepped between the two men, and he had a moment of fear when he realized that both men were a little more adept at their fighting than he was. A knock at the door had them all turning just as Elizabeth and Kim walked in.

"I've taken her to the castle to heal her. There isn't enough magic here to bring a basket of fruit to me." Elizabeth kissed his cheek and then Aaron's. Rythen sat on the sofa with Kim. "I've been thinking this over and all this nonsense must stop. Whether or not you use magic will not change the outcome. He's a monster, and putting a stop to doing what you love most will not change his mind."

"I am not a monster!" Elizabeth raised a brow at Rythen when he thundered at her. Even Kim looked at him as if she'd never seen him before. "I'm not. I've a job to do. And the sooner we can put it all behind us the better—"

"Behind us? Like the old newspapers, you think?" Kim stood up and glared down at him. "You plan to take the only person in the world who ever meant anything to me, and you think I should simply put it all behind me because you say so? You are a monster if you think that's all it takes. You talk of us being together, of spending our lifetimes together, and you're going to take her away from me. I don't know how I'm supposed to look at you and not think that had you some kind of…if you'd had a heart that I'd still have her."

Rythen stood up and reached for Kim, but she backed away. "You read the contract too. You know I've no choice in the—"

"Everyone has a choice. Just some of us refuse to see them." Kim turned to him. "You said that you'd help me if I asked. Is that still true?"

"It is." Logan watched Rythen as he moved to touch Kim, but she turned on him just before he touched her.

"Don't. I swear to you if you touch me again…I don't know what I'll do, but you do and I'll do something." Rythen looked at him as Kim continued speaking to him. "I'd like for you to set a meeting up with Morriganna. I'd like to have a word with her."

"You will not." They both ignored Rythen as Logan tried to think how he could fix this. He'd told Lizzy last night that this would happen, and she'd told him to give her one more day. She had a plan. The only thing he could see coming of this was a very unhappy woman and a pissed off being.

"I can, but you should think about what you're going to be doing. To have this relationship severed could mean great consequences for you both." Kim glanced at Rythen, then looked at him as he continued. "Once broken, there can never be any going back."

Lifting her chin, Kim nodded. He had called Morriganna last night and asked her about breaking the bond between Rythen and Kim, and she said she'd get back to him. He'd not heard anything since, and wondered if she was hiding from the problem. He knew that he would be if he could. Mathew came into the room just before he could say anything.

"Mom said to tell you that dinner will be in ten minutes, and if you're late she's going to castrate you." Logan had to cover his mouth as his son looked at Aaron. "She's sure moody lately. I'm almost looking forward to going back to school tomorrow."

"It's like that with women. When you take away something they love, they tend to take it out on the ones that are left behind. It doesn't really matter if they're the ones that ripped it from their hearts, but you have to simply be there for her." Aaron stood up and took Mathew's hand. "How about you and I go and see the new shipment of books that came in? I understand you and your brothers are reading them nightly. Good for you all. I think I might...."

Their voices faded away as they moved away from the room, and the door clicked shut behind them. Logan almost wished he could go too, but the couple in the room needed to hear what else he'd found out.

"You break this bond with Rythen and you'll go back to what you were. You'll be a human again and your memories...all of them...will be gone." Kim looked at Elizabeth, and Logan knew that she'd already told her. "You won't remember any of us or the things that happened to you. Josh will still be dead and you'll still have no job, but you'll not remember how it happened."

"I know. I don't think...I don't think there is anything I'll want to remember after she's gone." Logan almost looked at Rythen. He wanted to see if what Kim said had any effect on him, but was afraid to see nothing there.

When she nodded and left the room, Logan sat in his chair. He'd contact the witch after everyone left him.

"She's going to just cut us apart." Logan didn't say anything to Rythen, not entirely sure what to say. "How can she just throw this all away without even considering what we could have?"

"The same way you have, I would imagine." Elizabeth kissed Logan on the cheek as she made her way to the door as well. She turned back to Rythen just before she left. "I'm not going to see you at all between now and the time you end my life. I would appreciate it if you'd just leave me to my family. If you do happen to be in the same house I wish to go to, I would very much like it if you left. These people are my family, and I'll not have you there making them uncomfortable."

Rythen nodded, and Elizabeth left. It was a long, quiet few moments before either of them spoke. Logan just wanted him to go away, but he could see that Rythen wasn't going to give him what he wanted. When he stood in front of the window and stared out, Logan could almost feel sorry for him. Almost.

"I've lived my whole life thinking that I knew the way things would go. I've never once been questioned on what I thought. I've never had anyone say no to me. And I've certainly never had anyone that would rather forget everything rather than remember one moment of life with me." Logan didn't comment. What could he say anyway but "you've brought this all on yourself"? "If you don't mind, young man, I'd like to spend the rest of the time in your lairs below grounds. I shan't come above ground until it is time for me…."

He didn't finish, but Logan understood. "I've no problem with it if you don't. But I, too, would appreciate it if you stayed away from my family. We're to host a dinner party this evening, and there will be a great many people here that would cause you harm. I'm sure you will understand when I also point out that I won't raise a hand to help you if they do."

"Yes. I understand." He left him after that, and Logan was still sitting at his desk when the Sisters Three appeared before him. He was no happier to see them than he was knowing that Rythen was in his basement levels. They sat on the furniture, and before he could say anything, Clotho laughed.

"You've been reading into this all wrong, my dear boy. Perhaps you should read the part of her having a child again." The contract appeared in his hand, and he looked at her. "Read it. And if you have any questions, I should hope you know that I cannot answer them."

"I guessed as not." He waved the contract at them as he continued. "I love the old bat. I'm sure you know that, and I'm pretty sure you three do as well. Is there nothing that can be done about this?"

Lachesis laughed this time and told him to read. "You'll see a great many things that you missed before. Oh, and here are these papers as well. For some reason they ended up at our address instead of the intended person. Would you see that Elizabeth gets them?"

Logan nodded and watched them for several minutes. None of them spoke again but kept watching him. Finally giving up, he looked at the contract again. He was reading the page again when he looked up. There on his desk were the contract papers that Elizabeth had signed for Kim.

"I've no idea what you're talking about. You know that, right? What I'd really like to do is go downstairs and have dinner with my family." Clotho nodded. "Then I want to read them a story before the nanny takes them to the castle so they won't have to be here during the party. I'm afraid it will be a sad event for them."

"Yes, family is so wonderful, isn't it?" Logan nodded. "And the way Lizzy took your son to her heart…well, I was just telling my sisters that it's as if she'd given birth to him, they're so close. I bet he even thinks of her as his mother."

"He does." Logan knew he should have been getting something, but his mind was full of the things he wanted to do. "And the other boys too. They have already started calling her mom."

"As they should." The three of them stood up as one and smiled at him. "We know that you're not this dense, so we'll leave you to it."

They disappeared in a poof of smoke, and he was left with an eddy big enough to have papers drift to the floor. Bending to pick them up, he nearly fell to his knees when he saw it.

"You could have said something," he shouted to the empty room. The soft giggling had him smile. Things were about to get very fun from now on.

~~~

She opened her eyes and looked around. The man standing against the wall seemingly asleep didn't frighten her, but she also knew that she should know him. Not until she sat up and he looked at her did she remember his name.

"Rythen, my creator." He nodded at her and smiled. "I've been awake before now, haven't I?"

"No. This is your first time. How do you feel?" She moved her body off the long table and staggered slightly. When he touched her to keep her from falling, she felt a
~~~

current run along her skin much akin to the inner magic that ran all over her. She smiled at him.

"I feel as if I have just woke from a long sleep." He laughed at her, and she felt foolish. "I guess that's what has happened, is it not?"

"I would say that is true." She moved around the room touching the things that she knew what they were, their uses, but no memory of her ever seeing them before. He watched her the entire time without saying a word.

"I think I should like to go outside of here." He nodded but made no move to follow her. When the door opened before she touched it, she felt a small twinge of something, then let it go. He followed her but said nothing.

"I'm magic." He said she was. "And I'll rule all the magic in the world forever. No one will have as much power as me. Do you think that wise?"

"I would have thought so. What makes you believe it isn't?" She thought about it and realized that she should have someone govern her and told him so.

"They would be able to gainsay me if they think that I was to get out of hand. My head bigger than my magic." He nodded but said nothing. She decided that she'd create a being, or beings, that would help her in this. "I would also like to have a place of my own. A place I can…that no one can come to if I do not wish it."

"A place other than here?" She nodded. "That's up to you. You can do as you wish with your magic, so long as there are no problems that I must come and see to. I have created you so that I may rest. It has…I would say that it's drained me making you, but it's more than that. It has taken a great deal more than just my magic to make you."

"And who am I?" He looked at her oddly. "I am the queen, I understand that. You're Rythen, creator of magic, but who am I?"

"You wish a name in addition to the title I gave you?" She nodded. "Very well, what would you like to be called?"

"I don't know just yet. I shall think on it." She turned and left him there as she made her way into the fields behind the tiny house they'd been in. Lifting her arms to the sky, she felt what she needed to do and set about creating the kingdom that all would see. It would be theirs as well as hers, a place where they might seek refuge if things got bad.

"You will live there then?" She didn't answer him. No, she thought, she wouldn't live there. It was for the people. She would have a home…elsewhere. And it would be simple in comparison. "The people, where do you think they will come from? This place is simply where I have come to create you when there was no privacy on earth."

"I shall call it Molavonta. It will simply mean haven to all that need it." The walk around the fields tired the man, and she sat with him in the field. There was a small glen there, and she walked over to the area where some of the smallest creatures she ruled were sitting as well.

"You are the new queen." She nodded and sat down, making sure that Rythen was still comfortable in his rest. "You will rule us with magic as well as your love?"

"I will." The first faerie flew to her lap and looked up at her. "What will you be called, my child?"

"I was created to wake the flowers for you so that they were the first thing you saw in the morn, and put them to rest when the night comes." She looked around the field of flowers, then back at the girl. "We each have an assignment, but we weary of never getting a good rest. What say you about this?"

"Can you procreate?" The faerie looked at Rythen before she shook her head no. "Why is that?"

"He thinks that if our number is low we will work harder for you. But I fear it has made us hate you even before we met you." She could see that. Without anyone to help they'd be harmed from the overload. "I should like a child or two before I'm worn to nothing."

Touching the faerie's face, she felt the power run through her to the small being. The smile that she gave her back made her feel as if she'd been given a gift rather than her bestowing one upon her. She started to ask the being what her name was, but she spoke first.

"My name is Genese. I shall serve you for all my days." She nodded. "What shall we call you, my lady?"

"Elizabeth." The name made her feel like it was the right choice, and the little faerie nodded before flying away. Elizabeth stood up and went to the man and watched over him until he woke. When he did, she told him her name.

"Elizabeth? I like it. We have a few more things to go over before I take my leave. One is the contract." Elizabeth nodded. "It is important that you rule with an iron fist or the others will take all from you."

"My lady?" Elizabeth woke with a start. The faerie flying just above her was staring at her as if she'd never seen her before. "My lady? Are you well?"

"Yes, Genese, I am well. Sad, as you can well imagine, but well." She looked around the room and noticed that Phillip was gone. She wondered where he was when he walked into their room.

"We are to leave soon. I think this to be a grand party, don't you?" She nodded, the lump in her throat almost too much to talk around. "I think that Logan and the others will be very brave this night. I know that young Mathew has been working on a gift for us."

"He told me." She got up to dress and felt the weight of the memory on her heart. She wished she could go back and do things over, but it was much too late for that. Pulling her favorite gown to her cheek, she burst into tears. Phillip held her in his arms until she got them under control.

"I'm all right now." He held her just a bit longer, and she loved him all the more for it. By the time they were ready to go, she had a grip on her emotions, but her heart was heavy.

As soon as they entered the house, Mathew pulled her along to see what he'd been doing. She was going to die tomorrow and that was all Elizabeth could think about. It wasn't until Sara and Mel gave her a hug that she lost it. Sobbing again, she let them lead her to Logan's office, where they sat down. Embarrassed, Elizabeth fussed at them when both Lizzy and Savannah came in with Andi and Kim.

"I'm an old fool." None of them, of course, agreed with her, and she sat with them for several minutes before she started to speak. But before she could, Logan and Aaron came in, along with Rythen. She wanted to punch him in the nose, but Logan asked her to have a seat.

"I have some bad news, I'm afraid," Rythen said. Elizabeth felt her world tumble to a halt as they all sat down. Here it was—she was going to die right now.

CHAPTER 15

Rythen had been told before coming in this room that he was to keep his mouth shut unless spoken to. He wanted to beg them all to forgive him, but he was pretty sure that if he tried that, each of them would try to murder him. He'd fucked up. There was no other way to put it, and now…he feared now it was too late. He sat near the fireplace so that he could see his Kim, and she wouldn't even look at him.

"I've been doing some research. And since it has come to my attention that this stupidity is going to happen no matter what, I turned my focus to something more. And as such, I have a few questions to ask first." He handed Elizabeth an envelope, and they all watched as she opened it. "Did you sign that on the night that Kim was brought into the hospital?"

"I did. They said that they needed someone to pay the bills, as they had no insurance information for her." She started to hand them back, but Logan shook his head. "I have paid the bill, I assure you. When I didn't get the required paperwork, I went there on my own and paid it."

"You did. And what I want you to remember is what the nurse said to you when you were asked to sign the papers. Or in this case, Aaron, what did he tell you they wanted when you signed the paper?"

Elizabeth looked around the room, and Rythen had a feeling she was trying to see how this would get Kim into trouble. She stood up then and glared at Logan. Rythen nearly laughed, but he was afraid she'd turn her anger on him.

"He said that they need someone to be responsible for her. And if you think to make her pay me back, so help me I will beat you within an inch of your long life. To think I was going to miss you more than—" Logan cut Elizabeth off with a quick kiss. "Whatever was that for, young man?"

"You remembered." She looked as bewildered as the rest of the room, and Logan cleared this throat as he handed out some papers to everyone in the room. "This is a copy of part of the contract between Rythen and Elizabeth. I'd like for you all to read it if you don't mind."

Rythen looked down at the pages handed to him and nodded. Then he stood up. Christ. It was right there. He must have looked strange, because after a few minutes, Aaron asked him if he was ailing. It was all he could do not to jump for joy. Rythen looked at Logan.

"You're a good man." Logan bowed and smiled at him. "I wish I had had someone as you all those years ago. I might have turned out to be a better man. At least a smarter one."

"You might have, but I sincerely doubt it." Mel handed the papers back to Logan as he continued. "So what? We tried to fix this. There is no child other than me. I don't know what you wanted to come of this, but it's much too late for them to have a child."

"No, it's not." Logan nodded to him, and Rythen smiled at Mel as he continued with Logan's permission. "Don't you see? They do have a child. Or, at least Elizabeth does."

No one said anything, but he could feel their confusion. He thought about clearing it up for them, but Aaron suddenly jumped from his chair and picked Elizabeth up, swinging her around the room.

"You have a child. She's a bit on the older side, but you have a child. And I, for one, am the happiest uncle in the world." Elizabeth put her hand to his head as if to feel if he were feverish. "I'm not ill, you old bat, but you might be now. Don't you see? You took responsibility for her. For Kim. And when you paid the bill, you as good as adopted her. She's your child."

They all turned to look at him, and Rythen smiled. He felt as if a great weight had been lifted from his shoulders. Taking the contract from Logan, he tore it up into small pieces and tossed it into the air.

"The contract is specific about the time and the date. And as such I cannot go back now and change it. So, that being said...." Rythen bowed before his creation. "Elizabeth, Queen of all magick, I grant you the gift of life so that you may spend your days with your daughter, Kim Craft."

Rythen looked around the room as they celebrated. Kim sat there staring at him so long that he nearly asked her what was wrong, but he didn't. And he didn't belong there either. Instead of joining them, he bowed once again, this time before her, and disappeared. It was time for him to go.

His things were lying on the bed. Rythen was putting the last of his things into his bag when he heard someone knock at the door. He was both surprised and pleased to see Draco there. He bid the man welcome.

"I see you leave us." Rythen only nodded. He expected the man to be thrilled but saw that he looked saddened.

"She will be back. Elizabeth, I mean. There was some wording to the contract, and Logan saved the day. She will reign as queen so long as she wishes."

"I thought that might be the case. She has a responsibility to the child and should be able to see her training through." Rythen wasn't even surprised that he knew it already. The man probably knew all along. "I have come to see if you'd like to fly with me. You said you might enjoy it. And seeing that you're leaving, I thought we'd have one more."

Rythen nodded and moved toward the door. "I flew with your sire, you know. He was a good man. A great father and husband as well. We all have learned a thing or two about him in that respect. His mate loved him to distraction."

"Aye, she did. My mother still misses him, I think. He died in the other world, and when she passed of a broken heart…well, I don't think she ever truly died without him there beside her." Rythen used his considerable power to find the old dragon. And when he located him, Rythen smiled.

"I can have him brought here if you'd like. I know we would need the permission of Mel…the queen, but I can manage it if she says yes." Draco looked at him with tears in his eyes, and Rythen caught one before it fell. The tear turned to a diamond as soon as it fell into his palm. "This will make a lovely monument to him, I think."

"Or a beautiful bauble for your own mate." Rythen looked up at the old dragon. "You will have her again, I think. Her heart will seek what her mind does not yet realize it misses."

"I'm sure you're wrong." The next tear that fell from Draco's eyes was a sapphire. This one he caught and handed to him. Rythen took it and held it to the sun to look at its purity. "This will be worth a great deal on earth. Mayhap I will take them to her. She will need something to get by on, and it should fetch a few dollars."

"And you think that because you've said so, I'll take whatever it is that you're holding?" Rythen turned to see Kim standing behind him. She looked as beautiful as the gem he held in his hand and just as hard. "What? You suddenly have nothing to say for yourself?"

"I thought you'd be enjoying the party." They both turned when Draco sighed heavily. He was such a fearsome creature and yet gentle, too. "What?"

"You should have your head examined. She comes to see you, not banter about a party she left to see you." The shove to his back nearly had him tumble to the ground, and he might have had Kim not caught him before he fell. "Go and find a nice glen to play in. You will see much growth if you only find the right place."

When she turned to walk away, Rythen nearly cried out for her to stop. But the time for demands was over. It was time for him to ask things. He stepped beside her as they turned toward the field that they'd all repaired.

"I was told that in a week the faeries will have their hands full with picking the fruit and other things that now grow here. Some of the things that they are finding are seedlings that hadn't been seen since the forest was destroyed." Rythen hadn't heard that and told her so.

"Mel said that the forest has been dead for a very long time. She said that it was too much for her to do alone and that you'd done most of the work."

"I had a great deal of help." And now that he wasn't full of his own self-worth, he could admit that he'd had a great deal of help. "I think that Elizabeth deserves the credit. Had she been the leader I had hoped she'd be, then no one would have come to help her when she asked."

Kim nodded as they stood on the edge of the tree line. The trees had tripled since he'd been there last, and he remarked on that, too. Kim didn't say anything, and he found himself at a loss for words. When she turned to him, he could see her hurt.

"You would have left me, wouldn't you? It's no less than I deserve after the way I treated you, but I would have said goodbye." He tried to wrap his mind around what she was saying, but she continued before he could. "I could have made you very happy if not for the way you bossed me around all the time. I'm not going to let a man do that to me again."

"And you shouldn't." She nodded and turned to the forest again. Taking a chance, he moved up behind her and put his hands on her shoulders. When she didn't jerk away, he felt his heart pounding in his chest. "I was a fool."

"You're not going to get a disagreement from me on that score." He turned her then and looked into her eyes. He could see her love there and was almost afraid to speak. "You hurt me. Not with your claws, though that was enough, but you broke my heart when you dismissed me so much."

"I was a fool." She touched her fingers to his forehead, and he closed his eyes. "If you'd give me a chance, I'd very much like to take you out again."

"No." He looked down at her, and she smiled. "Not that I don't think we could find a restaurant that will allow us to come inside, but I don't think I'd like to share you with anyone just now."

"Share me?" She nodded. "And why would you have to share me, pray tell? Do you like me, Kim?"

"No." Rythen tried his best not to let his pain show on his face, but he was sure it was there for her to see. Before he could tell her he was sorry she felt that way, that over the course of the last few days he'd fallen in love with her, she said, "I don't just like you, Rythen, creator of magic, but I think I might love you."

~~~

When he didn't say anything, she turned again to the woods. Elizabeth had told her that she needed him. And as much as she wanted to tell her she didn't, Kim found that she really did need him. And not just to irritate her either. He caught up with her just as she was coming to the small lake that sat a mile or so in.

"You're in love with me. How can you say that after the way I've treated you?" She wasn't sure what to say, because she'd not been all that nice to him either. As she sat on the ground near the water, she pulled off her boot and socks. She might just drown herself if this failed too.

"I said I might. Don't get your underwear in a twist. I still might not." The water was cool over her feet, and she could see tiny fish just below the surface. "You should have stuck around. After you left, Duncan brought out—"

She was suddenly on her back, and Rythen was over her. Before she could figure out if he was going to strangle
~~~

her or not, he kissed her. Christ, she'd missed him. As he deepened the kiss, she wrapped her hands around his shoulders to pull him closer. He lifted his head just as she was wrapping her ankles around his hips.

"I'm going to make love to you right here if you'll allow it." She nodded, and he smiled at her. "But first I have something I'd like to ask you."

"Yes." She laughed when he did. "If you're going to ask me if I'm okay with making love out in the open with you, I will be." He shook his head at her.

"No, that's not what I was going say. But it's good to know that you're willing to try it." He rocked into her pussy and felt his cock thicken. She moaned when he did it again. "You're distracting me."

"Yes, I know. Please make love to me." He nodded, then shook his head. When he made no move to take her, she rolled him to his back and sat up over him. "I will have to do it then. I want to finish what we started in the restaurant before we were so rudely interrupted."

She closed her eyes and thought of them both naked. When he cupped her breast, she looked down at him and knew that she'd done it right. Moving back over his thigh, she wrapped her hand around him and fisted him. Leaning forward, she licked the tiny hole there before taking him into her mouth. He nearly gagged her when he rocked upward. But when she swallowed him, she moaned as well.

"Christ, love." He continued to rock upward until she cupped his balls. Then his entire body stilled, and she looked up at him, letting his cock go with a small pop sound. "I want to…nay, that's not right, I need to fuck you. Come inside of you."

He pulled her forward, and she guided his cock into her pussy. He took her breath away when he rolled her to her back and slammed deeply. Her body arched up to take him deeper as he pulled her ass tighter against him.

"Come, love. I want to feel your pussy milk me." Kim cried out when he slide his finger along her ass and pressed against her hole. "I know you were hurt here once, but I'd never harm you. The thought of fucking you here, coming deep in this tight hole, makes my body ache to take you."

Her body seemed to catch fire. She wanted him there as well. Taking her like an animal was hard while they were out here. Kim felt his teeth scrape along her throat, and she knew a new kind of need. The thought of him biting her, drinking from her, had her own fangs drop in response. As soon as he sank his fangs into her throat, she came apart, her body erupting in a climax that took her breath away.

His command for her to come again had her screaming. She tore into his shoulder with her fangs and tasted his blood as it filled her mouth. Sucking hard on the wound, she felt his cum fill her, and her body detonated again. This time she felt her world shatter as she cried out. As darkness took her, she felt a connection like she'd never felt before. They weren't just a couple, she thought, but one person. Her eyes slid closed when he fell atop her.

The next time she opened her eyes, she realized she was in bed. Where the bed was, she had no idea, but Rythen rolled to her then, and she didn't care. Wrapping her arms around him, she held him to her as he settled beside her. She snuggled tightly against his body and heard him laugh.

"I could get very used to this." She nodded, just not ready to talk just yet. "Did you know that we've never made love like that before? What I mean is, we've never made love, period. It was not anything like I thought it would be."

She lifted her head a little and looked at him. She wasn't really sure what he meant. He held out this hand, and she nearly jumped out of the bed when she saw what he was holding.

"Where on earth did you get that? Did you steal that from Draco?" She touched her finger to the baseball-sized sapphire and felt its warmth. "Is it real?"

"It is. And I didn't get it on earth. Draco gave it to me, both of them." She looked at him and wondered where the dragon would get such a treasure. "It's his tear."

"Tear?" She took the gem when he handed it to her. "I thought dragon's tears turned to diamonds, not sapphires. I mean, had you asked me several weeks ago if I thought that was true, I would have said there is no such thing as dragons. But now I know there are all sorts of things that I didn't know existed." He handed her the diamond as well, this one much bigger than the sapphire.

She weighed the stones in her hand and was amazed at their weight. When she tried to hand them back to Rythen, he told her they were hers.

"I want to have the sapphire broken up and a ring made for you. It would be our wedding rings." She looked at him when he said wedding. "You don't wish to marry me?"

"No. I mean yes." She took a deep breath. "I want to marry you, but don't break this up. It's too…I don't know, perfect for that."

"Well, they're yours to do with whatever you wish." Hers. He might as well have handed her the moon. It was the first thing she'd owned in her entire life. She was going to think of something great to do with it.

CHAPTER 16

"What do you mean, it's for the building? I can't take this." Aaron looked at Logan. He needed the man's help with this, and he sat there all smug. Young people today had no respect for their elders. When he burst out laughing, Aaron knew a new kind of aggression. "You should at least hide the fact that you're reading my mind."

"And what would be the fun in that? As for you being my elder? Face it, Aaron, everyone is young comparatively speaking." He sat up in his chair and picked up the large diamond. The thing had to weigh at least ten pounds, and Aaron was sure that the thing would fetch billions if someone were to cut it correctly.

"I want the three buildings on Jackson and the parking garage across from them." Aaron looked at Kim, trying to gauge how serious she was. There was something different about her yet....

"You're breeding." She looked at him when he suddenly stood. "Good Christ, you're going to have a child. How the hell did this happen?"

Logan laughed again, and the door opening behind him was the only thing that saved him from strangling the man. The rest of the Black team walked in and took seats. Kim looked slightly nervous, but she held herself well. He wanted to pursue this thing with her having a child, but he decided later, after they were alone. Bradley came to her and hugged her tightly, as did the other. It wasn't until they were all seated that Kim went to the large easel she'd brought in.

"The three buildings on Jackson have been sitting idle for nearly four years. I'd like to purchase them, as well as the parking garage across the street. As far as we've been able to tell, there are no liens on them and no projects slated to go there for now. The tax abatement you have gotten on the buildings will expire in another six years, and then you'll have to sell or use. I want them." Kim turned over the first page of her large pad of paper, and Aaron could see that she'd enlisted the help of Aric on her project. He'd know her artwork anywhere. "The first stages of the renovation will begin as soon as we sign off."

"And how did you find out about the tax abatement? Have you been snooping in minds when you shouldn't?" Colin popped Kyle on the head when he spoke.

"Behave. She's making a good point." Colin leaned back and waved her to continue, and she smiled at him. Colin had always had a way with women. And even with a mate, he still could charm them into nearly everything.

"As I was saying, the renovations would begin almost immediately. The second part of the project—" The door opened again, and Aaron heard Kim say "Thank goodness" before the mates to the men in the room stepped in. Lizzy kissed Kim on the cheek and sat down next to her.

"Should we know what's going on?" Everyone looked at him when no one answered Bradley's question. He had no idea and looked at Sara. She nodded his attention to Kim again.

"We're going to use the buildings. Our company…we don't have a classy name like you guys do yet, but we're working on it. We're forming a company to bring new business to the area. Not like you guys are, but shops for entertainment." She flushed again when Colin winked. Aaron took the file that Lizzy handed him as she picked up where Kim had left off.

"The first part of the buildings are the three here. We're going to tear down one of them to make room for the open courtyard. There will be live entertainment in the summer at lunchtimes as well as one night on the weekend." He looked at the drawings and could see that they'd put a great deal of thought into this. "The Middling Building will be outfitted to have shops on the bottom two levels using the staircase that is there. The man we had looking at it told us that it's made of mahogany and very sturdy."

"The upper two levels…." Another set of pictures was handed out by Shade as she picked up the conversation. "Will be changed into studios. Not apartments, but actual studios. Aric said that with the space and lighting we could easily have six artists per floor at any given time. This will be different than the artisan building we have near the school, in that this one will be for visiting artists and families. That's what we'd use the third through fifth floors for…apartments for them."

"Wait." Logan stood up and spread the pictures he'd been handed on the large conference table. There were perhaps thirty of them, each of them done so well and with enough detail that Aaron could already see the project completed. Sara handed Logan another stack of pictures, and these were added to the groups. Each of them gathered around the table to look them over.

"When did you come up with this?" Kyle was looking at the pictures when he asked, and then looked at Kim when no one answered him. "Kim? When did you guys come up with this?"

"The day I met Mr. Gibson there. I was nervous…I was really nervous, and to pass the time I…we started talking about how the building could be amazing for a place to shop. Once we started gathering ideas, the rest fell into place." She pointed to the picture that showed the entire project in place. "If you don't sell us the buildings, we'll simply find another spot. But our thinking is that with all the businesses you guys have in the area, women would come with their mates if they thought they might have things to do. We haven't had a lot of time to come up with a solid plan, but we'd talked about a large theater as well as a convention center for others to host things."

"I'd say if you came up with this on short notice, then I'm looking forward to what you could do with more time." Aaron agreed with Logan. There was a great deal of thought and planning in this.

"What do ye think of children? There donna seem to be much in the way for them here." Aaron walked to where Colin was pointing and could see that he was right. All the shops they had drawn were mostly for women. Very little, if anything, to entice a man to enter. "Do you think to have a day care?"

He'd been joking, of course, but Sara stood up and pointed to one of the later pictures. "There is a day center here. It's not just for young children, but for teenagers as well. A place that will be manned only during shop hours, and with a doctor and nurse on staff while there are children on site. We've talked it over and, while there will be some infants of their own born soon, the day center is not going to take infants. It requires too many man hours for them."

"How do you plan to pay for this?" Aaron wasn't going to take the diamond. He knew as well as Logan did that it would not only fund the entire thing they'd planned, but would run it for decades to come. He looked around the room when no one answered him.

"We're going to help." Elizabeth appeared in the room, along with the Fates, Mel, and Morriganna. The witches and the Fates sat down, and Elizabeth went to the pictures. "Very lovely, my dear. I knew you could do this."

"With magic, you mean?" Aaron snorted at Elizabeth when she nodded. "And just how will that work? You know that the government doesn't really have a space to check for magical entity on their forms."

"Don't be an ass, Aaron. That's not what we meant." Elizabeth laid a bag on the table in the middle of the pictures. From the sound it made when it hit the table, he'd bet it weighed fifty pounds. He was almost afraid to ask what was in it. "Tears. Smaller than the one that Kim gave you at first, but gems all the same."

Aaron went to the bag and dumped it. He was right, he didn't want to know. Lying there, twinkling up at them, was perhaps a thousand of the most beautiful gems he'd ever seen. Most of them were diamonds, but there were still as many colors and stones as there were in a box of the coloring crayons that he'd seen Mathew use. He looked at Mel when she cleared her throat.

"He would like us to name it for him. That's what he said…Draco died this morning." Aaron sat down hard. The rest of them said nothing as Mel continued. "He'd come to see me last night. He knew of this project, you see, and was happy that his tears were going to go toward making it happen for so many. After a while he told me that he was tired and that…he said that he wished to end his life. I begged him to stay, promised him so much. But it was Rythen…Rythen found his father, and Draco said he was at peace now and wished to die."

Aaron felt his heart break into so many pieces he knew that he'd never feel it beat the same again. Draco had come to mean so much to him and his family. He would miss him the most of all the creatures that lived at the castle. As they all seemed stunned by the news, Aaron knew that this project would go through even if he had to fund it all on his own. He stood up just as Phillip, James, and Rythen appeared in the room.

"We'd like to be a part of this project as well." Another bag was set on the table, and this one was bigger than the last. Kim picked up the diamond she'd given him and put it on the table with all the other gems.

"If you turn them down, Aaron Xavier MacManus, I shall never speak to you again." He smiled at Elizabeth. This wasn't really a threat because they'd been using it the entire time they'd known each other.

"Now you've made it nearly too tempting for me to want to go ahead with it." When she stood up, he hugged her to him. "I'm kidding you. I don't know how we can not sell the building now. We'll take a vote and see—"

"I say we sell." Bradley nodded to the rest of the men. "All who agree, raise your hands." Everyone raised their hands, including Phillip and James. Rythen pulled Kim into his arms and lifted her up. It was settled.

"And what shall we call this project of yours?" Everyone looked at Mel when Aaron asked. He'd only meant it to be a way to seal the deal, but he realized then that the name was as important, if not more so, than the project itself. She smiled at him. Oh, he didn't think he was going to like this.

"How about simply 'Draco'?" He smiled at her. He'd been thinking she'd say something like "Dragon's Tears" or "Draco's Last Stand." Both said what it was but were such…well, downers.

Aaron sat down and watched the rest of them as they started pooling their knowledge together. Elizabeth sat next to him, and he glanced at her. She had something to say to him, and Aaron had a feeling it was going to piss him off.

"Why is it you always think the worst of me?" He looked at her, and she smiled. "I guess I deserve that. We've been frienemies for a long time, haven't we?"

He laughed at her use of the words. They had been friends and at times enemies, too. He pulled her hand to his mouth and kissed it. He really did like the old bag.

"I've been thinking about the day at the hospital. The day you asked me to sign for her. Why did you do that?" He looked at her, then at Kim. "You knew then, didn't you?"

"I'd been...let's just call it 'coached' into making it happen." He looked at her again. "You love her, don't you? Like your own child? I wasn't told incorrectly, was I?"

"No. You weren't. And I do love her. She is…I was going to say she is saving my life, but we both know that you did that all on your own." Elizabeth looked at him, and he waited. "You saved my life."

"No. You did." He shifted on his chair and tried to think how to tell her what had been in his heart for too long without being said. "I love you too, as I'm sure you know. But the way you are with everyone…I don't just mean magic beings, but everyone. You're the kindest, most gentle person I know. You've the heart of a warrior when you need to have it, and more compassion in one finger than most people have in their entire body. I've never met a more giving and understanding woman, who could, in a heartbeat, come down on someone hard enough to have them pray for death."

"You make me sound like some avenging angel. When we both know that I am not." He grinned at her, and she slapped him. "I guess I just, like most people should, wanted to treat people as I wanted to be treated."

"Rythen told me he wanted you to rule with an iron fist, and that there were no gray areas when it came to ruling." He smiled at her again. "I'm very glad that you did things differently. I don't think…no, that's not true—I'm sure…that Mel would have been a much different queen had you been that way."

"She would have been like Sherman." Aaron nodded. He'd been thinking the same thing. "I remember the day that I had to rule against one of the families that went against all that I tried to instill in the world. The man and his family had been taking the faerie in the land and selling them to the highest bidder. Can you imagine what would have happened had there been Internet at that time? I would never have gotten as many as I did back. But I did lose a few of them, and to this day it still breaks my heart."

"What did you do to him?" He watched her face and knew that she hated the memory as much as she did what the man had done to her.

"His family was not without guilt. His mate had been the lure, and his mate's family was his couriers. The man would seal them up in a crock and have them delivered to earth. They would…some died in the crossover because the fool hadn't given them proper ventilation. And those that survived had been…scarred. Two of them, after they returned, decided to fade. The rest I put to work in jobs that would keep them away from others. He'd marked them, you see. So I marked him before having his head removed from his body."

"Marked them?" He thought about a faerie he'd seen at the castle a few times. Her name had been Honey. Her face had been cut, and he'd often wondered what had happened. "He cut into their faces so that they'd hide in the houses of the homes he sold them to."

"Yes. He told them that the way they looked someone would surely kill them. And if they died in the other world, in this world their bodies would never be returned to their families. I've only just located the last of the ones who hadn't made it."

Aaron knew that she'd not leave them behind. She was without a doubt the most wonderful person he knew. He took her hand again and held it. Kim looked at them, and he thought about her child.

"She's going to have a baby." Elizabeth nodded. He should have known she'd be aware of it. "I wonder if she will stay here with it, or will she and Rythen live in the castle?"

"Both, I would imagine. Rythen has enlisted the help of Logan in finding a house, and Mac is helping him find a job." She looked at him. "I don't suppose you have an opening in one of your many endeavors, do you?"

"Looking out for the son-in-law, are you?" She slapped him, and Aaron laughed. "I might. I can see him working with the women on this project better. He seems to have a hand in it already."

He did, too. Offering suggestions to them all and not getting the least bit upset when he was shot down. This Rythen, the man in love with his mate, was now someone he could like. Aaron was glad that the poker had been removed from his ass.

"Phillip and I are going away for a while." Aaron started to tell her no, that they'd miss them too much, but she continued before he could. "We need to find some time to be a couple again. It's been too long since we've had a long vacation. We were thinking about a cruise around the world."

"That would be great for the two of you." He could see them enjoying it. He wondered if Sara might enjoy a vacation, too. It wasn't as if they were not able to come and go as they pleased, but it would be nice to get away. Aaron decided to plan something very soon for them. He was startled out of his planning when a very large and heavy package landed on his lap.

"It's from Draco." Aaron looked at Elizabeth. "He was very fond of you for some reason, and wanted you to have this. I do believe I'm jealous. He only left me his favorite pillow."

He thought about waiting to open it, but Elizabeth asked him what it was. Tearing open the parchment, he stared at the contents for a long while before he threw back his head and laughed. It took him five minutes to get his mirth under control so he could tell her what it was.

"Is that…good God. He's given you a scale? Whatever will you do with that thing?" Aaron knew just what he was going to do with it, and was honored that he'd given it to him.

"I'm going to use it as a shield. We'd talked long ago about how I was in the service of a great many leaders, and he told me about his armor. We would talk for hours on the subject of how his armor was superior to anything I had ever used. He said that one day he'd give me one. But to give me one then would be certain death for him. He told me how it would leave a bare spot on his body, and someone would...he was forever fanciful that a dragon slayer would come and try to take him. I think he thought it to be a great idea."

Draco had been his friend, and Aaron would miss him forever. But with this, this gift of his, he felt as if his heart mended just a little.

"I shall miss him." Aaron nodded. "Whatever will I do when I go out to the fields and not see him there?"

"We'll have our memories." Elizabeth was called to settle something about the project, and Aaron watched them. This was his family. It mattered little that they were not all vampires, but they belonged to him. Mathew came to sit next to him, and Aaron knew real joy.

The other boys were coming around, but he thought they were still afraid of him. He smiled when he thought of the trip they were taking tomorrow, and he knew it was going to go a long way toward building their trust. What child wouldn't like to spend the day at a castle with every magical creature they'd ever heard of right there for them to see?

The love of his life came to sit near him, and he pulled her into his lap. Aaron couldn't believe his luck and held her all the tighter because he'd found her.

"I think we should go on a trip." He looked at Sara when she smiled down at him. "I was speaking to Grandmother, and she said she'd love to have us along.

But I declined. I told her that we were taking one ourselves."

"Have I told you lately how brilliant I think you are?" She kissed his nose, and he held her. "I was thinking that we should go to France. I'm sure there are any number of things a couple of old vampires like us could get into."

"Yes, and mostly I'd like for you to get inside of me." The whispered comment had his cock jump, and he stood up when she did. "What do you think? Will they even miss us?"

"I don't care." He picked her up once they exited the room. Taking the stairs three at a time, Aaron hurried them to their room. Before the door was even closed behind them, he had her naked, and as soon as she touched the bed, he was inside of her. "I love coming home with you, Sara. I love you with all my heart."

"And I you, Aaron. Forever and a day."

About the Author

Kathi Barton, author of the bestselling series Force of Nature, lives in Nashport, Ohio with her husband Paul. In addition to writing full time Kathi likes to spend time with her eight grandkids, three children and three children-in-laws. She writes to relax and have fun.

Her muse, a cross between Jimmy Stewart and Hugh Jackman brings them to life for her readers in a way that has them coming back time and again for more. Her favorite genre is paranormal romance with a great deal of spice. You can visit Kathi on line and drop her an email if you'd like. She loves hearing from her fans. aaronskiss@gmail.com.

Follow Kathi on her blog:
http://kathisbartonauthor.blogspot.com/

www.ingramcontent.com/pod-product-compliance
Lightning Source LLC
Chambersburg PA
CBHW022103170626
46808CB00002B/567

* 9 7 8 1 6 2 9 8 9 0 7 6 0 *